D1596080

THE
CONFESSION

WORLD CLASSICS IN LARGE PRINT

American Authors Series

The aim of World Classics in Large Print is
to make the most enduring and popular works of
literature available in comfortable softcover editions
printed in clear, easy-to-read large type.

THE CONFESSION

Mary Roberts Rinehart

The LARGE PRINT
BOOK COMPANY

SANBORNVILLE, NEW HAMPSHIRE

First published in 1917

Typeset in 16 point Adobe Caslon type

This edition of *The Confession*
by Mary Roberts Rinehart
published in September 2004
by
The Large Print Book Company
P.O. Box 970
Sanbornville, NH 03872-0970

THE
CONFESSION

CHAPTER I

I AM NOT A SUSCEPTIBLE WOMAN. I am objective rather than subjective, and a fairly full experience of life has taught me that most of my impressions are from within out rather than the other way about. For instance, obsession at one time a few years ago of a shadowy figure on my right, just beyond the field of vision, was later exposed as the result of a defect in my glasses. In the same way Maggie, my old servant, was during one entire summer haunted by church bells and considered it a personal summons to eternity until it was shown to be in her inner ear.

Yet the Benton house undeniably made me uncomfortable. Perhaps it was because it had remained unchanged for so long. The old horsehair chairs, with their shiny mahogany frames, showed by the slightly worn places in the carpet before them that they had not deviated an inch from their position for many years. The carpets—carpets that reached to the very baseboards and gave under one's feet with the yielding of heavy padding beneath—were bright under beds and wardrobes, while in the centers of the rooms they had faded into the softness of old tapestry.

Maggie, I remember, on our arrival moved a

chair from the wall in the library, and immediately put it back again, with a glance to see if I had observed her.

"It's nice and clean, Miss Agnes," she said. "A—I kind of feel that a little dirt would make it more homelike."

"I'm sure I don't see why," I replied, rather sharply, "I've lived in a tolerably clean house most of my life."

Maggie, however, was digging a heel into the padded carpet. She had chosen a sunny place for the experiment, and a small cloud of dust rose like smoke.

"Germs!" she said. "Just what I expected. We'd better bring the vacuum cleaner out from the city, Miss Agnes. Them carpets haven't been lifted for years."

But I paid little attention to her. To Maggie any particle of matter not otherwise classified is a germ, and the prospect of finding dust in that immaculate house was sufficiently thrilling to tide over the strangeness of our first few hours in it.

Once a year I rent a house in the country. When my nephew and niece were children, I did it to take them out of the city during school vacations. Later, when they grew up, it was to be near the country club. But now, with the children married and new families coming along, we were more concerned with dairies than with clubs, and I inquired more carefully about the neighborhood

cows than about the neighborhood golf-links. I
had really selected the house at Benton Station
because there was a most alluring pasture, with a
brook running through it, and violets over the
banks. It seemed to me that no cow with a
conscience could live in those surroundings and
give colicky milk.

Then, the house was cheap. Unbelievably
cheap. I suspected sewerage at once, but it seemed
to be in the best possible order. Indeed, new
plumbing had been put in, and extra bathrooms
installed. As old Miss Emily Benton lived there
alone, with only an old couple to look after her, it
looked odd to see three bathrooms, two of them
new, on the second floor. Big tubs and showers,
although little old Miss Emily could have bathed
in the washbowl and have had room to spare.

I faced the agent downstairs in the parlor, after
I had gone over the house. Miss Emily Benton
had not appeared and I took it she was away.

"Why all those bathrooms?" I demanded. "Does
she use them in rotation?"

He shrugged his shoulders.

"She wished to rent the house, Miss Blakiston.
The old-fashioned plumbing—"

"But she is giving the house away," I exclaimed.
"Those bathrooms have cost much more than she
will get out of it. You and I know that the price is
absurd."

He smiled at that. "If you wish to pay more,

you may, of course. She is a fine woman, Miss Blakiston, but you can never measure a Benton with any yard-stick but their own. The truth is that she wants the house off her hands this summer. I don't know why. It's a good house, and she has lived here all her life. But my instructions, I'll tell you frankly, are to rent it, if I have to give it away."

With which absurd sentence we went out the front door, and I saw the pasture, which decided me.

In view of the fact that I had taken the house for my grandnieces and nephews, it was annoying to find, by the end of June, that I should have to live in it by myself. Willie's boy was having his teeth straightened, and must make daily visits to the dentist, and Jack went to California and took Gertrude and the boys with him.

The first curious thing happened then. I wrote to the agent, saying that I would not use the house, but enclosing a check for its rental, as I had signed the lease. To my surprise, I received in reply a note from Miss Emily herself, very carefully written on thin note-paper.

Although it was years since I had seen her, the exquisite neatness of the letter, its careful paragraphing, its margins so accurate as to give the impression that she had drawn a faint margin line with a lead pencil and then erased it—all these were as indicative of Emily Benton as—

well, as the letter was not.

As well as I can explain it, the letter was impulsive, almost urgent. Yet the little old lady I remembered was neither of these things. "My dear Miss Blakiston," she wrote. "But I do hope you will use the house. It was because I wanted to be certain that it would be occupied this summer that I asked so low a rent for it.

"You may call it a whim if you like, but there are reasons why I wish the house to have a summer tenant. It has, for one thing, never been empty since it was built. It was my father's pride, and his father's before him, that the doors were never locked, even at night. Of course I can not ask a tenant to continue this old custom, but I can ask you to reconsider your decision.

"Will you forgive me for saying that you are so exactly the person I should like to see in the house that I feel I can not give you up? So strongly do I feel this that I would, if I dared, enclose your check and beg you to use the house rent free. Faithfully yours, Emily Benton."

Gracefully worded and carefully written as the letter was, I seemed to feel behind it some stress of feeling, an excitement perhaps, totally out of proportion to its contents. Years before I had met Miss Emily, even then a frail little old lady, her small figure stiffly erect, her eyes cold, her whole bearing one of reserve. The Bentons, for all their open doors, were known in that part of the country as "proud." I can remember, too, how when I was a young girl my mother had regarded the rare invitations to have tea and tiny cakes in the Benton parlor as commands, no less, and had taken the long carriage-ride from the city with complacency. And now Miss Emily, last of the family, had begged me to take the house.

In the end, as has been shown, I agreed. The glamor of the past had perhaps something to do with it. But I have come to a time of life when, failing intimate interests of my own, my neighbors' interests are mine by adoption. To be frank, I came because I was curious. Why, aside from a money consideration, was the Benton house to be occupied by an alien household? It was opposed to every tradition of the family as I had heard of it.

I knew something of the family history: the Reverend Thaddeus Benton, rector of Saint Bartholomew, who had forsaken the frame rectory near the church to build himself the substantial home now being offered me; Miss Emily, his daughter, who must now, I computed, be nearly seventy; and a son whom I recalled faintly as hardly bearing out the Benton traditions of solidity and rectitude.

The Reverend Mr. Benton, I recalled, had taken the stand that his house was his own, and having moved his family into it, had thereafter, save on great occasions, received the congregation individually or en masse, in his study at the church. A patriarchal old man, benevolent yet austere, who once, according to a story I had heard in my girlhood, had horsewhipped one of his vestrymen for trifling with the affections of a young married woman in the village!

There was a gap of thirty years in my knowledge of the family. I had, indeed, forgotten its very existence, when by the chance of a newspaper advertisement I found myself involved vitally in its affairs, playing providence, indeed, and both fearing and hating my role. Looking back, there are a number of things that appear rather curious. Why, for instance, did Maggie, my old servant, develop such a dislike for the place? It had nothing to do with the house. She had not seen it when she first refused to go. But her reluctance was evident from the beginning.

"I've just got a feeling about it, Miss Agnes," she said. "I can't explain it, any more than I can explain a cold in the head. But it's there."

At first I was inclined to blame Maggie's "feeling" on her knowledge that the house was cheap. She knew it, as she has, I am sure, read all my letters for years. She has a distrust of a bargain. But later I came to believe that there was something more to Maggie's distrust—as though perhaps a wave of uneasiness, spreading from some unknown source, had engulfed her.

Indeed, looking back over the two months I

spent in the Benton house, I am inclined to go even further. If thoughts carry, as I am sure they do, then emotions carry. Fear, hope, courage, despair—if the intention of writing a letter to an absent friend can spread itself half-way across the earth, so that as you write the friend writes also, and your letters cross, how much more should big emotions carry? I have had sweep over me such waves of gladness, such gusts of despair, as have shaken me. Yet with no cause for either. They are gone in a moment. Just for an instant, I have caught and made my own another's joy or grief.

The only inexplicable part of this narrative is that Maggie, neither a psychic nor a sensitive type, caught the terror, as I came to call it, before I did. Perhaps it may be explainable by the fact that her mental processes are comparatively simple, her mind an empty slate that shows every mark made on it.

In a way, this is a study in fear.

Maggie's resentment continued through my decision to use the house, through the packing, through the very moving itself. It took the form of a sort of watchful waiting, although at the time we neither of us realized it, and of dislike of the house and its surroundings. It extended itself to the very garden, where she gathered flowers for the table with a ruthlessness that was almost vicious. And, as July went on, and Miss Emily made her occasional visits, as tiny, as delicate as herself, I had a curious conclusion forced on me. Miss Emily returned her antagonism. I was slow to credit it. What secret and even unacknowledged opposition could there be between my downright Maggie and this little old aristocrat with her frail hands and the soft rustle of silk about her?

In Miss Emily, it took the form of—how strange a word to use in connection with her!—of furtive watchfulness. I felt that Maggie's entrance, with nothing more momentous than the tea-tray, set her upright in her chair, put an edge to her soft voice, and absorbed her. She was still attentive to what I said. She agreed or dissented. But back of it all, with her eyes on me, she was watching Maggie.

With Maggie the antagonism took no such subtle form. It showed itself in the second best instead of the best china, and a tendency to weak tea, when Miss Emily took hers very strong. And such was the effect of their mutual watchfulness and suspicion, such perhaps was the influence of the staid old house on me, after a time even that fact, of the strong tea, began to strike me as incongruous. Miss Emily was so consistent, so consistently frail and dainty and so—well, unspotted seems to be the word—and so gentle, yet as time went on I began to feel that she hated Maggie with a real hatred. And there was the strong tea!

Indeed, it was not quite normal, nor was I. For by that time the middle of July it was before I figured out as much as I have set down in five minutes—by that time I was not certain about the house. It was difficult to say just what I felt about the house. Willie, who came down over a Sunday early in the summer, possibly voiced it when he came down to his breakfast there.

"How did you sleep?" I asked.

"Not very well." He picked up his coffee-cup, and smiled over it rather sheepishly. "To tell the truth, I got to thinking about things—the furniture and all that," he said vaguely. "How many people have sat in the chairs and seen themselves in the mirror and died in the bed, and so on."

Maggie, who was bringing in the toast, gave a sort of low moan, which she turned into a cough.

"There have been twenty-three deaths in it in the last forty years, Mr. Willie," she volunteered. "That's according to the gardener. And more than half died in that room of yours."

"Put down that toast before you drop it, Maggie," I said. "You're shaking all over. And go out and shut the door."

"Very well," she said, with a meekness behind which she was both indignant and frightened. "But there is one word I might mention before I go, and that is—cats!"

"Cats!" said Willie, as she slammed the door.

"I think it is only one cat," I observed mildly. "It belongs to Miss Emily, I fancy. It manages to be in a lot of places nearly simultaneously, and Maggie swears it is a dozen."

Willie is not subtle. He is a practical young man with a growing family, and a tendency the last year or two to flesh. But he ate his breakfast thoughtfully.

"Don't you think it's rather isolated?" he asked finally. "Just you three women here?" I had taken Delia, the cook, along.

"We have a telephone," I said, rather loftily. "Although—" I checked myself. Maggie, I felt sure, was listening in the pantry, and I intended to give her wild fancies no encouragement. To utter a thing is, to Maggie, to give it life. By the mere use of the spoken word it ceases to be supposition and becomes fact.

As a matter of fact, my uneasiness about the house resolved itself into an uneasiness about the telephone. It seems less absurd now than it did then. But I remember what Willie said about it that morning on our way to the church.

"It rings at night, Willie," I said. "And when I go there is no one there."

"So do all telephones," he replied briskly. "It's their greatest weakness."

"Once or twice we have found the thing on the floor in the morning. It couldn't blow over or knock itself down."

"Probably the cat," he said, with the patient air of a man arguing with an unreasonable woman. "Of course," he added—we were passing the churchyard then, dominated by what the village called the Benton "mosolem"—"there's a chance that those dead-and-gone Bentons resent anything as modern as a telephone. It might be interesting to see what they would do to a victrola.

"I'm going to tell you something, Willie," I said. "I am *afraid* of the telephone."

He was completely incredulous. I felt rather ridiculous, standing there in the sunlight of that summer Sabbath and making my confession. But I did it.

"I am afraid of it," I repeated. "I'm desperately sure you will never understand. Because I don't. I can hardly force myself to go to it. I hate the very back corner of the hall where it stands, I—"

I saw his expression then, and I stopped, furious with myself. Why had I said it? But more important still, why did I feel it? I had not put it into words before, I had not expected to say it then. But the moment I said it I knew it was true. I had developed an *idée fixe*.

"I have to go downstairs at night and answer it," I added, rather feebly. "It's on my nerves, I think."

"I should think it is," he said, with a note of wonder in his voice. "It doesn't sound like you. A telephone!" But just at the church door he stopped me, a hand on my arm.

"Look here," he said, "don't you suppose it's because you're so dependent on the telephone? You know that if anything goes wrong with it, you're cut off, in a way. And there's another point you get all your news over it, good and bad." He had difficulty, I think, in finding the words he wanted. "It's—it's vital," he said. "So you attach too much importance to it, and it gets to be an obsession."

"Very likely," I assented. "The whole thing is idiotic, anyhow."

But—was it idiotic?

I am endeavoring to set things down as they seemed to me at the time, not in the light of subsequent events. For, if this narrative has any interest at all, it is a psychological one. I have said that it is a study in fear, but perhaps it would be more accurate to say that it is a study of the mental reaction of crime, of its effects on different minds, more or less remotely connected with it.

That my analysis of my impression; in the church that morning are not colored by subsequent events is proved by the fact that under cover of that date, July 16th, I made the following entry:

"Why do Maggie and Miss Benton distrust each other?"

I realized it even then, although I did not

consider it serious, as is evidenced by the fact that I follow it with a recipe for fruit gelatin, copied from the newspaper.

It was a calm and sunny Sunday morning. The church windows were wide open, and a butterfly came in and set the choir boys to giggling. At the end of my pew a stained-glass window to Carlo Benton—the name came like an echo from the forgotten past—sent a shower of colored light over Willie, turned my blue silk to most unspinsterly hues, and threw a sort of summer radiance over Miss Emily herself, in the seat ahead.

She sat quite alone, impeccably neat, even to her profile. She was so orderly, so well balanced, one stitch of her hand-sewed organdy collar was so clearly identical with every other, her very seams, if you can understand it, ran so exactly where they should, that she set me to pulling myself straight. I am rather casual as to seams.

After a time I began to have a curious feeling about her. Her head was toward the rector, standing in a sort of white nimbus of sunlight, but I felt that Miss Emily's entire attention was on our pew, immediately behind her. I find I can not put it into words, unless it was that her back settled into more rigid lines. I glanced along the pew. Willie's face wore a calm and slightly somnolent expression. But Maggie, in her far end—she is very high church and always attends—Maggie's eyes were glued almost fiercely to Miss Emily's back. And just then Miss Emily herself stirred, glanced up at the window, and turning slightly, returned Maggie's glance with one almost as malevolent. I have hesitated over that word. It seems strong now, but at the time it was the one that came into my mind.

When it was over, it was hard to believe that it had happened. And even now, with everything else clear, I do not pretend to explain Maggie's attitude. She knew, in some strange way. But she did not know that she knew—which sounds like nonsense and is as near as I can come to getting it down in words.

Willie left that night, the 16th, and we settled down to quiet days, and, for a time, to undisturbed nights. But on the following Wednesday, by my journal, the telephone commenced to bother me again. Generally speaking, it rang rather early, between eleven o'clock and midnight. But on the following Saturday night I find I have recorded the hour as 2 a.m.

In every instance the experience was identical. The telephone never rang the second time. When I went downstairs to answer it—I did not always go—there was the buzzing of the wire, and there was nothing else. It was on the twenty-fourth that I had the telephone inspected and reported in normal condition, and it is possibly significant that for three days afterward my record shows not a single disturbance.

But I do not regard the strange calls over the telephone as so important as my attitude to them. The plain truth is that my fear of the calls extended itself in a few days to cover the instrument, and more than that, to the part of the house it stood in. Maggie never had this, nor did she recognize it in me. Her fear was a perfectly simple although uncomfortable one, centering around the bedrooms where, in each bed, she nightly saw dead and gone Bentons laid out in all the decorum of the best linen.

On more than one evening she came to the library door, with an expression of mentally looking over her shoulder, and some such dialogue would follow:

"D'you mind if I turn the bed down now, Miss Agnes?"

"It's very early."

"S'almost eight." When she is nervous she cuts verbal corners.

"You know perfectly well that I dislike having the beds disturbed until nine o'clock, Maggie."

"I'm going out."

"You said that last night, but you didn't go."

Silence.

"Now, see here, Maggie, I want you to overcome this feeling of—" I hesitated—"of fear. When you have really seen or heard something, it will be time enough to be nervous."

"Humph!" said Maggie on one of these occasions, and edged into the room. It was growing dusk. "It will be too late then, Miss Agnes. And another thing. You're a brave woman. I don't know as I've seen a braver. But I notice you keep away from the telephone after dark."

The general outcome of these conversations was that, to avoid argument, I permitted the preparation of my room for the night at an earlier and yet earlier hour, until at last it was done the moment I was dressed for dinner.

It is clear to me now that two entirely different sorts of fear actuated us. For by that time I had to acknowledge that there was fear in the house. Even Delia, the cook, had absorbed some of Maggie's terror; possibly traceable to some early impressions of death which connected themselves with a four-post bedstead.

Of the two sorts of fear, Delia's and Maggie's symptoms were subjective. Mine, I still feel, were objective.

It was not long before the beginning of August, and during a lull in the telephone matter, that I began to suspect that the house was being visited at night.

There was nothing I could point to with any certainty as having been disturbed at first. It was a matter of a book misplaced on the table, of my sewing-basket open when I always leave it closed, of a burnt match on the floor, whereas it is one of my orderly habits never to leave burnt matches around. And at last the burnt match became a sort of clue, for I suspected that it had been used to light one of the candles that sat in holders of every sort, on the top of the library shelves.

I tried getting up at night and peering over the banisters, but without result. And I was never sure as to articles that they had been moved. I remained in that doubting and suspicious halfway ground that is worse than certainty. And there was the matter of motive. I could not get away from that. What possible purpose could an intruder have, for instance, in opening my sewing-basket or moving the dictionary two inches on the center table?

Yet the feeling persisted, and on the second of August I find this entry in my journal:

Right-hand brass, eight inches; left-hand brass, seven inches; carved-wood—Italian—five and three quarter inches each; old glass on mantelpiece—seven inches. And below this, dated the third: Last night, between midnight and daylight, the candle in the glass holder on the right side of the mantel was burned down one and one-half inches.

I should, no doubt, have set a watch on my nightly visitor after making this discovery—and one that was apparently connected with it—

nothing less than Delia's report that there were candledroppings over the border of the library carpet. But I have admitted that this is a study in fear, and a part of it is my own.

I was afraid. I was afraid of the night visitor, but, more than that, I was afraid of the fear. It had become a real thing by that time, something that lurked in the lower back hall waiting to catch me by the throat, to stop my breath, to paralyze me so I could not escape. I never went beyond that point.

Yet I am not a cowardly woman. I have lived alone too long for that. I have closed too many houses at night and gone upstairs in the dark to be afraid of darkness. And even now I can not, looking back, admit that I was afraid of the darkness there, although I resorted to the weak expedient of leaving a short length of candle to burn itself out in the hall when I went up to bed.

I have seen one of Willie's boys waken up at night screaming with a terror he could not describe. Well, it was much like that with me, except that I was awake and horribly ashamed of myself.

On the fourth of August I find in my journal the single word "flour." It recalls both my own cowardice at that time, and an experiment I made. The telephone had not bothered us for several nights, and I began to suspect a connection of this sort: when the telephone rang, there was no night visitor, and *vice versa*. I was not certain.

Delia was setting bread that night in the kitchen, and Maggie was reading a ghost story from the evening paper. There was a fine sifting of flour over the table, and it gave me my idea. When I went up to bed that night, I left a powdering of flour here and there on the lower floor, at the door into the library, a patch by the table, and—going back rather uneasily—one near the telephone.

I was up and downstairs before Maggie the next morning. The patches showed trampling. In the doorway they were almost obliterated, as by the trailing of a garment over them, but by the fireplace there were two prints quite distinct. I knew when I saw them that I had expected the marks of Miss Emily's tiny foot, although I had not admitted it before. But these were not Miss Emily's. They were large, flat, substantial, and one showed a curious marking around the edge that—It was my own! The marking was the knitted side of my bedroom slipper. I had, so far as I could tell, gone downstairs, in the night, investigated the candles, possibly in darkness, and gone back to bed again.

The effect of the discovery on me was—well undermining. In all the uneasiness of the past few weeks I had at least had full confidence in myself. And now that was gone. I began to wonder how

much of the things that had troubled me were
real, and how many I had made for myself.

To tell the truth, by that time the tension was
almost unbearable. My nerves were going, and
there was no reason for it. I kept telling myself
that. In the mirror I looked white and anxious,
and I had a sense of approaching trouble. I caught
Maggie watching me, too, and on the seventh I
find in my journal the words: "Insanity is often
only a formless terror."

On the Sunday morning following that I found
three burnt matches in the library fireplace, and
one of the candles in the brass holders was almost
gone. I sat most of the day in that room,
wondering what would happen to me if I lost my
mind. I knew that Maggie was watching me, and
I made one of those absurd hypotheses to myself
that we all do at times. If any of the family came,
I would know that she had sent for them, and
that I was really deranged! It had been a long day,
with a steady summer rain that had not cooled the
earth, but only set it steaming. The air was like
hot vapor, and my hair clung to my moist
forehead. At about four o'clock Maggie started
chasing a fly with a folded newspaper. She
followed it about the lower floor from room to
room, making little harsh noises in her throat
when she missed it. The sound of the soft thud of
the paper on walls and furniture seemed suddenly
more than I could bear.

"For heaven's sake!" I cried. "Stop that noise, Maggie." I felt as though my eyes were starting from my head.

"It's a fly," she said doggedly, and aimed another blow at it. "If I don't kill it, we'll have a million. There, it's on the mantel now. I never—"

I felt that if she raised the paper club once more I should scream. So I got up quickly and caught her wrist. She was so astonished that she let the paper drop, and there we stood, staring at each other. I can still see the way her mouth hung open.

"Don't!" I said. And my voice sounded thick even to my own ears. "Maggie—I can't stand it!"

"My God, Miss Agnes!"

Her tone brought me up sharply. I released her arm.

"I—I'm just nervous, Maggie," I said, and sat down. I was trembling violently.

I was sane. I knew it then as I know it now. But I was not rational. Perhaps to most of us come now and then times when they realize that some act, or some thought, is not balanced, as though, for a moment or an hour, the control was gone from the brain. Or—and I think this was the feeling I had—that some other control was in charge. Not the Agnes Blakiston I knew, but another Agnes Blakiston, perhaps, was exerting a temporary dominance, a hectic, craven, and hateful control.

That is the only outburst I recall. Possibly Maggie may have others stored away. She has a tenacious memory. Certainly it was my nearest approach to violence. But it had the effect of making me set a watch on myself.

Possibly it was coincidence. Probably, however, Maggie had communicated with Willie. But two days later young Martin Sprague, Freda Sprague's son, stopped his car in the drive and came in. He is a nerve specialist, and very good, although I can remember when he came down in his night drawers to one of his mother's dinner-parties.

"Thought I would just run in and see you, he said. "Mother told me you were here. By George, Miss Agnes, you look younger than ever."

"Who told you to come, Martie?" I asked.

"Told me? I don't have to be told to visit an old friend."

Well, he asked himself to lunch, and looked over the house, and decided to ask Miss Emily if she would sell an old Japanese cabinet inlaid with mother of pearl that I would not have had as a gift. And, in the end, I told him my trouble, of the fear that seemed to center around the telephone, and the sleep-walking.

He listened carefully.

"Ever get any bad news over the telephone?" he asked.

One way and another, I said I had had plenty of it. He went over me thoroughly, and was inclined to find my experience with the flour rather amusing than otherwise. "It's rather good, that," he said. "Setting a trap to catch yourself. You'd better have Maggie sleep in your room for a while. Well, it's all pretty plain, Miss Agnes. We bury some things as deep as possible, especially if we don't want to remember that they ever happened. But the mind's a queer thing. It holds on pretty hard, and burying is not destroying. Then we get tired or nervous—maybe just holding the thing down and pretending it is not there makes us nervous—and up it pops, like the ghost of a buried body, and raises hell. You don't mind that, do you?" he added anxiously. "It's exactly what those things do raise."

"But," I demanded irritably, "who rings the telephone at night? I daresay you don't contend that I go out at night and call the house, and then come back and answer the call, do you?"

He looked at me with a maddening smile.

"Are you sure it really rings?" he asked.

And so bad was my nervous condition by that time, so undermined was my self-confidence, that I was not certain! And this in face of the fact that it invariably roused Maggie as well as myself.

On the eleventh of August Miss Emily came to tea. The date does not matter, but by following the chronology of my journal I find I can keep my narrative in proper sequence.

I had felt better that day. So far as I could

determine, I had not walked in my sleep again, and there was about Maggie an air of cheerfulness and relief which showed that my condition was more nearly normal than it had been for some time. The fear of the telephone and of the back hall was leaving me, too. Perhaps Martin Sprague's matter-of-fact explanation had helped me. But my own theory had always been the one I recorded at the beginning of this narrative—that I caught and—well, registered is a good word— that I registered an overwhelming fear from some unknown source.

I spied Miss Emily as she got out of the hack that day, a cool little figure clad in a thin black silk dress, with the sheerest possible white collars and cuffs. Her small bonnet with its crepe veil was faced with white, and her carefully crimped gray hair showed a wavy border beneath it. Mr. Staley, the station hackman, helped her out of the surrey, and handed her the knitting-bag without which she was seldom seen. It was two weeks since she had been there, and she came slowly up the walk, looking from side to side at the perennial borders, then in full August bloom.

She smiled when she saw me in the doorway, and said, with the little anxious pucker between her eyes that was so childish, "Don't you think peonies are better cut down at this time of year?" She took a folded handkerchief from her bag and dabbed at her face, where there was no sign of dust to mar its old freshness. "It gives the lilies a better chance, my dear."

I led her into the house, and she produced a gay bit of knitting, a baby afghan, by the signs. She smiled at me over it.

"I am always one baby behind," she explained and fell to work rapidly. She had lovely hands, and I suspected them of being her one vanity.

Maggie was serving tea with her usual grudging reluctance, and I noticed then that when she was in the room Miss Emily said little or nothing. I thought it probable that she did not approve of conversing before servants, and would have let it go at that, had I not, as I held out Miss Emily's cup, caught her looking at Maggie. I had a swift impression of antagonism again, of alertness and something more. When Maggie went out, Miss Emily turned to me.

"She is very capable, I fancy."

"Very. Entirely too capable."

"She looks sharp," said Miss Emily. It was a long time since I had heard the word so used, but it was very apt. Maggie was indeed sharp. But Miss Emily launched into a general dissertation on servants, and Maggie's sharpness was forgotten.

It was, I think, when she was about to go that I asked her about the telephone.

"Telephone?" she inquired. "Why, no. It has always done very well. Of course, after a heavy snow in the winter, sometimes—"

She had a fashion of leaving her sentences unfinished. They trailed off, without any abrupt break.

"It rings at night."

"Rings?"

"I am called frequently and when I get to the phone, there is no one there."

Some of my irritation doubtless got into my voice, for Miss Emily suddenly drew away and stared at me.

"But—that is very strange. I—"

She had gone pale. I saw that now. And quite suddenly she dropped her knitting-bag. When I restored it to her, she was very calm and poised, but her color had not come back.

"It has always been very satisfactory," she said. "I don't know that it ever—"

She considered, and began again. "Why not just ignore it? If some one is playing a malicious trick on you, the only thing is to ignore it."

Her hands were shaking, although her voice was quiet. I saw that when she tried to tie the ribbons of the bag. And—I wondered at this, in so gentle a soul—there was a hint of anger in her tones. There was an edge to her voice.

That she could be angry was a surprise. And I found that she could also be obstinate. For we came to an impasse over the telephone in the next few minutes, and over something so absurd that I was non-plussed. It was over her unqualified refusal to allow me to install a branch wire to my bedroom.

"But," I expostulated, "when one thinks of the convenience, and—"

"I am sorry." Her voice had a note of finality. "I daresay I am old-fashioned, but—I do not like changes. I shall have to ask you not to interfere with the telephone."

I could hardly credit my senses. Her tone was one of reproof, plus decision. It convicted me of an indiscretion. If I had asked to take the roof off and replace it with silk umbrellas, it might have been justified. But to a request to move the telephone!

"Of course, if you feel that way about it," I said, "I shall not touch it."

I dropped the subject, a trifle ruffled, I confess, and went upstairs to fetch a box in which Miss Emily was to carry away some flowers from the garden.

It was when I was coming down the staircase that I saw Maggie. She had carried the hall candlesticks, newly polished, to their places on the table, and was standing, a hand on each one, staring into the old Washington mirror in front of her. From where she was she must have had a full view of Miss Emily in the library. And Maggie was bristling. It was the only word for it.

She was still there when Miss Emily had gone,

blowing on the mirror and polishing it. And I took her to task for her unfriendly attitude to the little old lady.

"You practically threw her muffins at her," I said. "And I must speak again about the cups—"

"What does she come snooping around for, anyhow?" she broke in. "Aren't we paying for her house? Didn't she get down on her bended knees and beg us to take it?"

"Is that any reason why we should be uncivil?"

"What I want to know is this," Maggie said truculently. "What right has she to come back, and spy on us? For that's what she's doing, Miss Agnes. Do you know what she was at when I looked in at her? She was running a finger along the baseboard to see if it was clean! And what's more, I caught her at it once before, in the back hall, when she was pretending to telephone for the station hack."

It was that day, I think, that I put fresh candles in all the holders downstairs. I had made a resolution like this—to renew the candles, and to lock myself in my room and throw the key over the transom to Maggie. If, in the mornings that followed, the candles had been used, it would prove that Martin Sprague was wrong, that even foot-prints could lie, and that some one was investigating the lower floor at night. For while my reason told me that I had been the intruder, my intuition continued to insist that my sleepwalking was a result, not a cause. In a word, I had gone downstairs, because I knew that there had been and might be again, a night visitor.

Yet, there was something of comedy in that night's precautions, after all.

At ten-thirty I was undressed, and Maggie had, with rebellion in every line of her, locked me in. I could hear her, afterwards running along the hall to her own room and slamming the door. Then, a moment later, the telephone rang.

It was too early, I reasoned, for the night calls. It might be anything, a telegram at the station, Willie's boy run over by an automobile, Gertrude's children ill. A dozen possibilities ran through my mind.

And Maggie would not let me out!

"You're not going downstairs," she called, from a safe distance.

"Maggie!" I cried, sharply. And banged at the door. The telephone was ringing steadily. "Come here at once."

"Miss Agnes," she beseeched, "you go to bed and don't listen. There'll be nothing there, for all your trouble," she said, in a quavering voice. "It's nothing human that rings that bell."

Finally, however, she freed me, and I went down the stairs. I had carried down a lamp, and my nerves were vibrating to the rhythm of the bell's shrill summons. But, strangely enough, the fear had left me. I find, as always, that it is difficult to put into words. I did not relish the excursion to the lower floor. I resented the jarring sound of the bell. But the terror was gone.

I went back to the telephone. Something that was living and moving was there. I saw its eyes, lower than mine, reflecting the lamp like twin lights. I was frightened, but still it was not the *fear*. The twin lights leaped forward—and proved to be the eyes of Miss Emily's cat, which had been sleeping on the stand!

I answered the telephone. To my surprise it was Miss Emily herself, a quiet and very dignified voice which apologized for disturbing me at that hour, and went on:

"I feel that I was very abrupt this afternoon, Miss Blakiston. My excuse is that I have always feared change. I have lived in a rut too long, I'm afraid. But of course, if you feel you would like to move the telephone, or put in an upstairs instrument, you may do as you like."

She seemed, having got me there, unwilling to ring off. I got a curious effect of reluctance over the telephone, and there was one phrase that she repeated several times.

"I do not want to influence you. I want you to do just what you think best."

The fear was entirely gone by the time she rang off. I felt, instead, a sort of relaxation that was most comforting. The rear hall, a cul-de-sac of nervousness in the daytime and of horror at night, was suddenly transformed by the light of my lamp into a warm and cheerful refuge from the darkness of the lower floor. The purring of the cat, comfortably settled on the telephone-stand, was as cheering as the singing of a kettle on a stove. On the rack near me my garden hat and an old Paisley shawl made a grotesque human effigy.

I sat back in the low wicker chair and surveyed the hallway. Why not, I considered, do away now with the fear of it? If I could conquer it like this at midnight, I need never succumb again to it in the light.

The cat leaped to the stand beside me and stood there, waiting. He was an intelligent animal, and I am like a good many spinsters. I am not more fond of cats than other people, but I understand them better. And it seemed to me that he and I were going through some familiar program, of which a part had been neglected. The cat neither sat nor lay, but stood there, waiting.

So at last I fetched the shawl from the rack and made him a bed on the stand. It was what he had been waiting for. I saw that at once. He walked onto it, turned around once, lay down, and closed his eyes.

I took up my vigil. I had been the victim of a fear I was determined to conquer. The house was quiet. Maggie had retired shriveled to bed. The cat slept on the shawl.

And then—I felt the fear returning. It welled

up through my tranquillity like a flood, and swept me with it. I wanted to shriek. I was afraid to shriek. I longed to escape. I dared not move. There had been no sound, no motion. Things were as they had been.

It may have been one minute or five that I sat there. I do not know. I only know that I sat with fixed eyes, not even blinking, for fear of even for a second shutting out the sane and visible world about me. A sense of deadness commenced in my hands and worked up my arms. My chest seemed flattened.

Then the telephone bell rang.

The cat leaped to his feet. Somehow I reached forward and took down the receiver.

"Who is it?" I cried, in a voice that was thin, I knew, and unnatural.

The telephone is not a perfect medium. It loses much that we wish to register but, also, it registers much that we may wish to lose. Therefore when I say that I distinctly heard a gasp, followed by heavy difficult breathing, over the telephone, I must beg for credence. It is true. Some one at the other end of the line was struggling for breath.

Then there was complete silence. I realized, after a moment, that the circuit had been stealthily cut, and that my conviction was verified by Central's demand, a moment later, of what number I wanted. I was, at first, unable to answer her. When I did speak, my voice was shaken.

"What number, please?" she repeated, in a bored tone. There is nothing in all the world so bored as the voice of a small town telephone-operator.

"You called," I said.

"Beg y'pardon. Must have been a mistake," she replied glibly, and cut me off.

CHAPTER II

IT MAY BE SAID, and with truth, that so far I have recorded little but subjective terror, possibly easily explained by my occupancy of an isolated house, plus a few unimportant incidents, capable of various interpretations. But the fear was, and is today as I look back, a real thing. As real—and as difficult to describe—as a chill, for instance. A severe mental chill it was, indeed.

I went upstairs finally to a restless night, and rose early, after only an hour or so of sleep. One thing I was determined on—to find out, if possible, the connection between the terror and the telephone. I breakfasted early, and was dressing to go to the village when I had a visitor, no other than Miss Emily herself. She looked fluttered and perturbed at the unceremonious hour of her visit—she was the soul of convention—and explained, between breaths as it were, that she had come to apologize for the day before. She had hardly slept. I must forgive her. She had been very nervous since her brother's death, and small things upset her.

How much of what I say of Miss Emily depends on my later knowledge, I wonder? Did I notice then that she was watching me furtively, or is it only on looking back that I recall it? I do recall it—the hall door open and a vista of smiling garden beyond, and silhouetted against the sunshine, Miss Emily's frail figure and searching, slightly uplifted face. There was something in her eyes that I had not seen before—a sort of exaltation. She was not, that morning, the Miss Emily who ran a finger along her baseboards to see if we dusted them.

She had walked out, and it had exhausted her. She breathed in little gasps.

"I think," she said at last, "that I must telephone for Mr. Staley, I am never very strong in hot weather."

"Please let me call him, for you, Miss Emily." I am not a young woman, and she was at least sixty-five. But, because she was so small and frail, I felt almost a motherly anxiety for her that morning.

"I think I should like to do it, if you don't mind. We are old friends. He always comes promptly when I call him."

She went back alone, and I waited in the doorway. When she came out, she was smiling, and there was more color in her face.

"He is coming at once. He is always very thoughtful for me."

Now, without any warning, something that had been seething since her breathless arrival took shape in my mind, and became—suspicion. What if it had been Miss Emily who had called me the second time to the telephone, and having established the connection, had waited, breathing hard for—what?

It was fantastic, incredible in the light of that brilliant summer day. I looked at her, dainty and exquisite as ever, her ruchings fresh and white, her very face indicative of decorum and order, her wistful old mouth still rather like a child's, her eyes, always slightly upturned because of her diminutive height, so that she had habitually a look of adoration.

"One of earth's saints," the rector had said to me on Sunday morning. "A good woman, Miss Blakiston, and a sacrifice to an unworthy family."

Suspicion is like the rain. It falls on the just and on the unjust. And that morning I began to suspect Miss Emily. I had no idea of what.

On my mentioning an errand in the village she promptly offered to take me with her in the Staley hack. She had completely altered in manner. The strain was gone. In her soft low voice, as we made our way to the road, she told me the stories of some of the garden flowers.

"The climbing rose over the arch, my dear," she said, "my mother brought from England on her wedding journey. People have taken cuttings from it again and again, but the cuttings never thrive. A bad winter, and they are gone. But this one has lived. Of course now and then it freezes down."

She chattered on, and my suspicions grew more and more shadowy. They would have gone, I think, had not Maggie called me back with a grocery list.

"A sack of flour," she said, "and some green vegetables, and—Miss Agnes, that woman was down on her knees beside the telephone!—and bluing for the laundry, and I guess that's all."

The telephone! It was always the telephone. We drove on down the lane, eyed somnolently by spotted cows and incurious sheep, and all the way Miss Emily talked. She was almost garrulous. She asked the hackman about his family and stopped the vehicle to pick up a peddler, overburdened with his pack. I watched her with amazement. Evidently this was Mr. Staley's Miss Emily. But it was not mine.

But I saw mine, too, that morning. It was when I asked the hackman to put me down at the little telephone building. I thought she put her hand to her throat, although the next moment she was only adjusting the ruching at her neck.

"You—you have decided to have the second telephone put in, then?"

I hesitated. She so obviously did not want it installed. And was I to submit meekly to the fear again, without another effort to vanquish it?

"I think not, dear Miss Emily," I said at last, smiling at her drawn face. "Why should I disturb your lovely old house and its established order?"

"But I want you to do just what you think best," she protested. She had put her hands together. It was almost a supplication.

As to the strange night calls, there was little to be learned. The night operator was in bed. The manager made a note of my complaint, and promised an investigation, which, having had experience with telephone investigations, I felt would lead nowhere. I left the building, with my grocery list in my hand.

The hack was gone, of course. But—I may have imagined it—I thought I saw Miss Emily peering at me from behind the bonnets and hats in the milliner's window.

I did not investigate. The thing was enough on my nerves as it was.

Maggie served me my luncheon in a sort of strained silence. She observed once, as she brought me my tea, that she was giving me notice and intended leaving on the afternoon train. She had, she stated, holding out the sugar-bowl to me at arm's length, stood a great deal in the way of irregular hours from me, seeing as I would read myself to sleep, and let the light burn all night, although very fussy about the gas-bills. But she had reached the end of her tether, and you could grate a lemon on her most anywhere, she was that covered with goose-flesh.

"Goose-flesh about what?" I demanded. "And either throw the sugar to me or come closer."

"I don't know about what," she said sullenly. "I'm just scared."

And for once Maggie and I were in complete harmony. I, too, was "just scared."

We were, however, both of us much nearer a solution of our troubles than we had any idea of. I say solution, although it but substituted one mystery for another. It gave tangibility to the intangible, indeed, but I can not see that our situation was any better. I, for one, found myself in the position of having a problem to solve, and no formula to solve it with.

The afternoon was quiet. Maggie and the cook were in the throes of jelly-making, and I had picked up a narrative history of the county, written most pedantically, although with here and there a touch of heavy lightness, by Miss Emily's father, the Reverend Samuel Thaddeus Benton.

On the fly-leaf she had inscribed, "Written by my dear father during the last year of his life, and published after his death by the parish to which he had given so much of his noble life."

The book left me cold, but the inscription warmed me. Whatever feeling I might have had about Miss Emily died of that inscription. A devoted and self-sacrificing daughter, a woman both loving and beloved, that was the Miss Emily of the dedication to *Fifty Years in Bolivar County*.

In the middle of the afternoon Maggie appeared, with a saucer and a teaspoon. In the saucer she had poured a little of the jelly to test it, and she was blowing on it when she entered. I put down my book.

"Well!" I said. "Don't tell me you're not dressed yet. You've just got about time for the afternoon train."

She gave me an imploring glance over the saucer.

"You might just take a look at this, Miss Agnes," she said. "It jells around the edges, but in the middle—"

"I'll send your trunk tomorrow," I said, "and you'd better let Delia make the jelly alone. You haven't much time, and she says she makes good jelly."

She raised anguished eyes to mine.

"Miss Agnes," she said, "that woman's never made a glass of jelly in her life before. She didn't even know about putting a silver spoon in the tumblers to keep 'em from breaking."

I picked up *Bolivar County* and opened it, but I could see that the hands holding the saucer were shaking.

"I'm not going, Miss Agnes," said Maggie. (I had, of course, known she would not. The surprising thing to me is that she never learns this fact, although she gives me notice quite regularly. She always thinks that she is really going, until the last.) "Of course you can let that woman make the jelly, if you want. It's your fruit and sugar. But I'm not going to desert you in your hour of need."

"What do I need?" I demanded. "Jelly?"

But she was past sarcasm. She placed the saucer on a table and rolled her stained hands in her apron.

"That woman," she said, "what was she doing under the telephone stand?"

She almost immediately burst into tears, and it was some time before I caught what she feared. For she was more concrete than I. And she knew now what she was afraid of. It was either a bomb or fire.

"Mark my words, Miss Agnes," she said, "she's going to destroy the place. What made her set out and rent it for almost nothing if she isn't? And I know who rings the telephone at night. It's her."

"What on earth for?" I demanded as ungrammatical and hardly less uneasy than Maggie.

"She wakes us up, so we can get out in time. She's a preacher's daughter. More than likely she draws the line at bloodshed. That's one reason.

Maybe there's another. What if by pressing a button somewhere and ringing that bell, it sets off a bomb somewhere?"

"It never has," I observed dryly.

But however absurd Maggie's logic might be, she was firm in her major premise. Miss Emily had been on her hands and knees by the telephone-stand, and had, on seeing Maggie, observed that she had dropped the money for the hackman out of her glove.

"Which I don't believe. Her gloves were on the stand. If you'll come back, Miss Agnes, I'll show you how she was."

We made rather an absurd procession, Maggie leading with the saucer, I following, and the cat, appearing from nowhere as usual, bringing up the rear. Maggie placed the jelly on the stand, and dropped on her hands and knees, crawling under the stand, a confused huddle of gingham apron, jelly-stains, and suspicion.

"She had her head down like this," she said, in rather a smothered voice. "I'm her, and you're me. And I says: 'If it's rolled off somewhere I'll find it next time I sweep, and give it back to you.' Well, what d'you think of that! Here it is!"

My attention had by this time been caught by the jelly, now unmistakably solidifying in the center. I moved to the kitchen door to tell Delia to take it off the fire. When I returned, Maggie was digging under the telephone battery-box with a hair-pin and muttering to herself.

"Darnation!" she said, "it's gone under!"

"If you do get it," I reminded her, "it belongs to Miss Emily."

There is a curious strain of cupidity in Maggie. I have never been able to understand it. With her own money she is as free as air. But let her see a chance for illegitimate gain, of finding a penny on the street, of not paying her fare on the cars, of passing a bad quarter, and she is filled with an unholy joy. And so today. The jelly was forgotten. Terror was gone. All that existed for Maggie was a twenty-five~cent piece under a battery-box.

Suddenly she wailed: "It's gone, Miss Agnes. It's clear under!"

"Good heavens, Maggie! What difference does it make?"

"W'you mind if I got the ice-pick and unscrewed the box?"

My menage is always notoriously short of tools.

I forbade it at once, and ordered her back to the kitchen, and after a final squint along the carpet, head flat, she dragged herself out and to her feet.

"I'll get the jelly off," she said, "and then maybe a hat pin'll reach it. I can see the edge of it."

A loud crack from the kitchen announced that cook had forgotten the silver spoon, and took Maggie off on a jump. I went back to the library and *Bolivar County*, and, I must confess, to a nap in my chair.

I was roused by the feeling that some one was staring at me. My eyes focused first on the icepick, then, as I slowly raised them, on Maggie's face, set in hard and uncompromising lines.

"I'd thank you to come with me," she said stiffly.

"Come where?"

"To the telephone.

I groaned inwardly. But, because submission to Maggie's tyranny has become a firm habit with me, I rose. I saw then that she held a dingy quarter in one hand.

Without a word she turned and stalked ahead of me into the hall. It is curious, looking back and remembering that she had then no knowledge of the significance of things, to remember how hard and inexorable her back was. Viewed through the light of what followed, I have never. been able to visualize Maggie moving down the hall. It has always been a menacing figure, rather shadowy than real. And the hall itself takes on grotesque proportions, becomes inordinately long, an infinity of hall, fading away into time and distance.

Yet it was only a moment, of course, until I stood by the telephone. Maggie had been at work. The wooden box which covered the battery-jars had been removed, and lay on its side. The battery-jars were uncovered, giving an effect of mystery unveiled, a sort of shamelessness, of destroyed illusion.

Maggie pointed. "There's a paper under one of the jars," she said. "I haven't touched it, but I know well enough what it is."

I have not questioned Maggie on this point, but I am convinced that she expected to find a sort of final summons, of death's visiting-card, for one or the other of us.

The paper was there, a small folded scrap, partially concealed under a jar.

"Them prints was there, too," Maggie said, non-committally.

The box had accumulated the fluctuant floating particles of months, possibly years—lint from the hall carpet giving it a reddish tinge. And in this light and evanescent deposit, fluttered by a breath, fingers had moved, searched, I am tempted to say groped, although the word seems absurd for anything so small. The imprint of Maggie's coin and of her attempts at salvage were at the edge and quite distinct from the others.

I lifted the jar and picked up the paper. It was folded and refolded until it was not much larger than a thumb-nail, a rather stiff paper crossed with faint blue lines. I am not sure that I would have opened it—it had been so plainly in hiding, and was so obviously not my affair—had not Maggie suddenly gasped and implored me not to look at it. I immediately determined to examine it.

Yet, after I had read it twice, it had hardly made an impression on my mind. There are some things so incredible that the brain automatically rejects them. I looked at the paper. I read it with my eyes. But I did not grasp it.

It was not note paper. It was apparently torn from a tablet of glazed and ruled paper—just such paper, for instance, as Maggie soaks in brandy and places on top of her jelly before tying it up. It had been raggedly torn. The scrap was the full width of the sheet, but only three inches or so deep. It was undated, and this is what it said:

"To Whom it may concern: On the 30th day of May, 1911, I killed a woman (here) in this house. I hope you will not find this until I am dead.
(Signed) EMILY BENTON."

Maggie had read the confession over my shoulder, and I felt her body grow rigid. As for myself, my first sensation was one of acute discomfort—that we should have exposed the confession to the light of day. Neither of us, I am sure, had really grasped it. Maggie put a trembling hand on my arm.

"The brass of her," she said, in a thin, terrified voice. "And sitting in church like the rest of us. Oh, my God, Miss Agnes, put it back!"

I whirled on her, in a fury that was only an

outlet for my own shock.

"Once for all, Maggie," I said, "I'll ask you to wait until you are spoken to. And if I hear that you have so much as mentioned this—piece of paper, out you go and never come back."

But she was beyond apprehension. She was literal, too. She saw, not Miss Emily unbelievably associated with a crime, but the crime itself.

"Who d'you suppose it was, Miss Agnes?"

"I don't believe it at all. Some one has placed it there to hurt Miss Emily."

"It's her writing," said Maggie doggedly.

After a time I got rid of her, and sat down to think in the library. Rather I sat down to reason with myself.

For every atom of my brain was clamoring that this thing was true, that my little Miss Emily, exquisite and fine as she was, had done the thing she claimed to have done. It was her. own writing, thin, faintly shaded, as neat and as erect as herself. But even that I would not accept, until I had compared it with such bits of hers as I possessed, the note begging me to take the house, the inscription on the fly-leaf of *Fifty Years in Bolivar County.*

And here was something I could not quite understand. The writing was all of the same order, but while the confession and the inscription in the book were similar, letter for letter, in the note to me there were differences, a change in the "t" in Benton, a fuller and blacker stroke, a variation in the terminals of the letters—it is hard to particularize.

I spent the remainder of the day in the library, going out for dinner, of course, but returning to my refuge again immediately after. Only in the library am I safe from Maggie. By virtue of her responsibility for my wardrobe, she virtually shares my bedroom, but her respect for books she never reads makes her regard a library as at least semi-holy ground. She dusts books with more caution than china, and her respect for a family Bible is greater than her respect for me.

I spent the evening there, Miss Emily's cat on the divan, and the mysterious confession lying before me under the lamp. At night the variation between it and her note to me concerning the house seemed more pronounced. The note looked more like a clumsy imitation of Miss Emily's own hand. Or—perhaps this is nearer—as if, after writing in a certain way for sixty years, she had tried to change her style.

All my logic ended in one conclusion. She must have known the confession was there. Therefore the chances were that she had placed it there. But it was not so simple as that.

Both crime and confession indicated a degree of impulse that Miss Emily did not possess. I have entirely failed with my picture of Miss Emily if the word violence can be associated with her in any way. Miss Emily was a temple, clean swept, cold, and empty. She never acted on impulse. Every action, almost every word, seemed the result of thought and deliberation.

Yet, if I could believe my eyes, five years before she had killed a woman in this very house. Possibly in the very room in which I was then sitting.

I find, on looking back, that the terror must have left me that day. It had, for so many weeks, been so much a part of my daily life that I would have missed it had it not been for this new and engrossing interest. I remember that the long French windows of the library reflected the room like mirrors against the darkness outside, and that once I thought I saw a shadowy movement in one of them, as though a figure moved behind me. But when I turned sharply there was no one there, and Maggie proved to be, as usual after nine o'clock, shut away upstairs.

I was not terrified. And indeed the fear never returned. In all the course of my investigations, I was never again a victim of the unreasoning fright of those earlier days.

My difficulty was that I was asked to believe the unbelievable. It was impossible to reconstruct in that quiet house a scene of violence. It was equally impossible, in view, for instance, of that calm and filial inscription in the history of Bolivar County, to connect Miss Emily with it. She had killed a woman, forsooth! Miss Emily, of the baby afghans, of the weary peddler, of that quiet seat in the church.

Yet I knew now that Miss Emily knew of the confession; knew, at least, of something concealed in that corner of the rear hall which housed the telephone. Had she by chance an enemy who would have done this thing? But to suspect Miss Emily of an enemy was as absurd as to suspect her of a crime.

I was completely at a loss when I put out the lights and prepared to close the house. As I glanced back along the hall, I could not help wondering if the telephone, having given up its secret, would continue its nocturnal alarms. As I stood there, I heard the low growl of thunder and the patter of rain against the windows. Partly out of loneliness, partly out of bravado, I went back to the telephone and tried to call Willie. But the line was out of order.

I slept badly. Shortly after I returned I heard a door slamming repeatedly, which I knew meant an open window somewhere. I got up and went into the hall. There was a cold air coming from somewhere below. But as I stood there it ceased. The door above stopped slamming, and silence reigned again.

Maggie roused me early. The morning sunlight was just creeping into the room, and the air was still cool with the night and fresh-washed by the storm.

"Miss Agnes," she demanded, standing over me, "did you let the cat out last night?"

"I brought him in before I went to bed."

"Humph!" said Maggie. "And did I or did I not wash the doorstep yesterday?"

"You ought to know. You said you did."

"Miss Agnes," Maggie said, "that woman was in this house last night. You can see her footprints as plain as day on the doorstep. And what's more, she stole the cat and let out your mother's Paisley shawl."

Which statements, corrected, proved to be true. My old Paisley shawl was gone from the hallrack, and unquestionably the cat had been on the back doorstep that morning along with the milk bottles. Moreover, one of my fresh candles had been lighted, but had burned for only a moment or two.

That day I had a second visit from young Martin Sprague. The telephone was in working order again, having unaccountably recovered, and I was using it when he came. He watched me quizzically from a position by the newelpost, as I rang off.

"I was calling Miss Emily Benton," I explained, "but she is ill."

"Still troubled with telephobia?"

"I have other things to worry me, Martin," I said gravely, and let him into the library.

There I made a clean breast of everything I omitted nothing. The fear, the strange ringing of the telephone bell; the gasping breathing over it the night before; Miss Emily's visit to it. And, at last, the discovery.

He took the paper when I offered it to him, and examined it carefully by a window. Then he stood looking out and whistling reflectively. At last he turned back to the room.

"It's an unusual story," he said. "But if you'll give me a little time I'll explain it to you. In the first place, let go of the material things for a moment, and let's deal with minds and emotions. You're a sensitive person, Miss Agnes. You catch a lot of impressions that pass most people by. And, first of all, you've been catching fright from two sources."

"Two sources?"

"Two. Maggie is one. She hates the country. She is afraid of old houses. And she sees in this house only the ghosts of people who have died here."

"I pay no attention to Maggie's fears."

"You only think that. But to go further—you have been receiving waves of apprehension from another source—from the little lady, Miss Emily."

"Then you think—"

"Hold on," he said smiling. "I think she wrote that confession. Yes. As a matter of fact, I'm quite sure she did. And she has established a system of espionage on you by means of the telephone. If you had discovered the confession, she knew that there would be a change in your voice, in your manner. If you answered very quickly, as though you had been near the instrument, perhaps in the very act of discovering the paper—don't you get it? And can't you see how her terror affected you even over the wire? Don't you think that, if thought can travel untold distances, fear can? Of course."

"But, Martin!" I exclaimed. "Little Miss Emily a murderess."

He threw up his hands.

"Certainly not," he said. "You're a shrewd woman, Miss Agnes. Do you know that a certain type of woman frequently confesses to a crime she never committed, or had any chance of committing? Look at the police records— confessions of women as to crimes they could only have heard of through the newspapers! I would like to wager that if we had the newspapers of that date that came into this house, we would find a particularly atrocious and mysterious murder being featured—the murder of a woman."

"You do not know her," I maintained doggedly. And drew, as best I could, a sketch of Miss Emily, while he listened attentively.

"A pure neurasthenic type," was his comment. "Older than usual, but that is accountable by the sheltered life she has led. The little Miss Emily is still at heart a girl. And a hysterical girl."

"She has had enough trouble to develop her."

"Trouble! Has she ever had a genuine emotion? Look at this house. She nursed an old father in it, a bedridden mother, a paretic brother, when she should have been having children. Don't you see it, Miss Agnes? All her emotions have had to be mental. Failing them outside, she provided them for herself. This"—he tapped the paper in his hand—"this is one."

I had heard of people confessing to crimes they had never committed, and at the time Martin Sprague at least partly convinced me. He was so sure of himself. And when, that afternoon, he telephoned me from the city to say that he was mailing out some old newspapers, I knew quite well what he had found.

"I've thought of something else, Miss Agnes," he said. "If you'll look it up you will probably find that the little lady had had either a shock sometime before that, or a long pull of nursing. Something, anyhow, to set her nervous system to going in the wrong direction."

Late that afternoon, as it happened, I was enabled to learn something of this from a visiting neighbor, and once again I was forced to acknowledge that he might be right.

The neighbors had not been over cordial. I had gathered, from the first, the impression that the members of the Reverend Samuel Thaddeus Benton's congregation did not fancy an interloper among the sacred relics of the historian of Bolivar County. And I had a corroboration of that impression from my visitor of that afternoon, a Mrs. Graves.

"I've been slow in coming, Miss Blakiston," she said, seating herself primly. "I don't suppose you can understand, but this has always been the Benton place, and it seems strange to us to see new faces here."

I replied, with some asperity, that I had not been anxious to take the house, but that Miss Emily had been so insistent that I had finally done so.

It seemed to me that she flashed a quick glance at me.

"She is quite the most loved person in the valley," she said. "And she loves the place. It is—I cannot imagine why she rented the house. She is far from comfortable where she is."

After a time I gathered that she suspected financial stringency as the cause, and I tried to set her mind at rest.

"It cannot be money," I said. "The rent is absurdly low. The agent wished her to ask more, but she refused."

She sat silent for a time, pulling at the fingers of her white silk gloves. And when she spoke again it was of the garden. But before she left she returned to Miss Emily.

"She has had a hard life, in a way," she said. "It is only five years since she buried her brother, and her father not long before that. She has broken a great deal since then. Not that the brother—"

"I understand he was a great care."

Mrs. Graves looked about the room, its shelves piled high with the ecclesiastical library of the late clergyman.

"It was not only that," she said. "When he was—all right, he was an atheist. Imagine, in this house! He had the most terrible books, Miss Blakiston. And, of course, when a man believes there is no hereafter, he is apt to lead a wicked life. There is nothing to hold him back."

Her mind was on Miss Emily and her problems. She moved abstractedly toward the door.

"In this very hall," she said, "I helped Miss Emily to pack all his books into a box, and we sent for Mr. Staley—the hackman at the station, you know—and he dumped the whole thing into the river. We went away with him, and how she cheered up when it was done!"

Martin Sprague's newspapers arrived the next morning. They bore a date of two days before the date of the confession, and contained, rather triumphantly outlined in blue pencil, full details of the murder of a young woman by some unknown assassin. It had been a grisly crime, and the paper was filled with details of a most sensational sort.

Had I been asked, I would have said that Miss Emily's clear, slightly upturned eyes had never glanced beyond the merest headlines of such journalistic reports. But in a letter Martin Sprague set forth a precisely opposite view.

"You will probably find," he wrote, "that the little lady is pretty well fed up on such stuff. The calmer and more placid the daily life, the more apt is the secret inner one, in such a circumscribed existence, to be a thriller! You might look over the books in the house. There is a historic case where a young girl swore she had tossed her little brother to a den of lions (although there were no lions near, and little brother was subsequently found asleep in the attic) after reading *Fox's Book of Martyrs*. Probably the old gentleman has this joke book in his library."

I put down his letter and glanced around the room. Was he right, after all? Did women, rational, truthful, devout women, ever act in this strange manner? And if it was true, was it not in its own way as mysterious as everything else?

I was, for a time that day, strongly influenced by Martin Sprague's conviction. It was, for one thing, easier to believe than that Emily Benton had committed a crime. And, as if to lend color to his assertion, the sunlight, falling onto the dreary bookshelves, picked out and illuminated dull gilt letters on the brown back of a volume. It was *Fox's Book of Martyrs*!

If I may analyze my sensations at that time, they divided themselves into three parts. The first was fear. That seems to have given away to curiosity, and that at a later period, to an intense anxiety. Of the three, I have no excuse for the second, save the one I gave myself at the time— that Miss Emily could not possibly have done the thing she claimed to have done, and that I must prove her innocence to myself.

With regard to Martin Sprague's theory, I was divided. I wanted him to be right. I wanted him to be wrong. No picture I could visualize of little old Miss Emily conceivably fitted the type he had drawn. On the other hand, nothing about her could possibly confirm the confession as an actual one.

The scrap of paper became, for the time, my universe. Did I close my eyes, I saw it side by side with the inscription in *Fifty Years in Bolivar County*, and letter for letter, in the same hand. Did the sun shine, I had it in the light, examining it, reading it. To such a point did it obsess me that I refused to allow Maggie to use a tablet of glazed paper she had found in the kitchen table drawer to tie up the jelly-glasses. It seemed, somehow, horrible to me.

At that time I had no thought of going back five years and trying to trace the accuracy or falsehood of the confession. I should not have known how to go about it. Had such a crime been committed, how to discover it at this late day? Whom in all her sheltered life, could Miss Emily have murdered? In her small world, who could have fallen out and left no sign?

It was impossible, and I knew it. And yet—

Miss Emily was ill. The news came through the grocery boy, who came out every day on a bicycle, and teased the cat and carried away all the pears as fast as they ripened. Maggie brought me the information at luncheon.

"*She's* sick," she said.

There was only one person in both our minds those days.

"Do you mean really ill, or only—"

"The boy says she's breaking up. If you ask me, she caught cold the night she broke in here and took your Paisley shawl. And if you ask my advice, Miss Agnes, you'll get it back again before the heirs step in and claim it. They don't make them shawls nowadays, and she's as like as not to will it to somebody if you don't go after it."

"Maggie," I said quietly, "how do you know she has that shawl?"

"How did I know that paper was in the telephone-box?" she countered.

And, indeed, by that time Maggie had convinced herself that she had known all along there was something in the telephone battery-box.

"I've a sort of second sight, Miss Agnes," she added. And, with a shrewdness I found later was partially correct: "She was snooping around to see if you'd found that paper, and it came on to rain; so she took the shawl. I should say," said Maggie, lowering her voice, "that as like as not she's been in this house every night since we came."

That afternoon I cut some of the roses from the arch for Miss Emily, and wrapping them against the sun, carried them to the village. At the last I hesitated. It was so much like prying. I turned aside at the church intending to leave them there for the altar. But I could find no one in the parish house, and no vessel to hold them.

It was late afternoon. I opened a door and stepped into the old church. I knelt for a moment, and then sat back and surveyed the quiet building. It occurred to me that here one could obtain a real conception of the Benton family, and of Miss Emily. The church had been the realest thing in their lives. It had dominated them, obsessed them. When the Reverend Samuel Thaddeus died, they had built him, not a monument, but a parish house. When Carlo Benton died (however did such an ungodly name come to belong to a Benton?) Miss Emily according to the story, had done without fresh mourning and built him a window.

I looked at the window. It was extremely ugly,

and very devout. And under it was the dead man's name and two dates, 1860 and 1911.

So Carlo Benton had died the year Miss Emily claimed to have done a murder! Another proof, I reflected that Martin Sprague would say. He had been on her hands for a long time, both well and ill. Small wonder if little Miss Emily had fallen to imagining things, or to confessing them.

I looked at the memorial window once more, and I could almost visualize her gathering up the dead man's hateful books, and getting them as quickly as possible out of the house. Quite possibly there were unmentionable volumes among them—de Maupassant, perhaps Boccaccio. I had a distinct picture, too, of Mrs. Graves, lips primly set, assisting her with hands that fairly itched with the righteousness of her actions.

I still held the roses, and as I left the church I decided to lay them on some grave in the churchyard. I thought it quite likely that roses from the same arch had been frequently used for that purpose. Some very young grave, I said to myself, and found one soon enough, a bit of a rectangle of fresh earth, and a jarful of pansies on it. It lay in the shadow of the Benton mausoleum.

That was how I found that Carlo Benton had died on the 27th of May, 1911.

I cannot claim that the fact at the time had any

significance for me, or that I saw in it anything more than another verification of Martin Sprague's solution. But it enabled me to reconstruct the Benton household at the date that had grown so significant. The 30th would have probably been the day after the funeral. Perhaps the nurse was still there. He had had a nurse for months, according to Mrs. Graves. And there would have been the airing that follows long illness and death, the opened windows, the packing up or giving away of clothing, the pauses and silences, the sense of strangeness and quiet, the lowered voices. And there would have been, too, that remorseless packing for destruction of the dead atheist's books.

And some time, during that day or the night that followed, little Miss Emily claimed to have committed her crime.

I went home thoughtfully. At the gate I turned and looked back. The Benton Mausoleum was warm in the sunset, and the rose sprays lay, like outstretched arms, across the tiny grave.

Maggie is amazingly efficient. I am efficient myself, I trust, but I modify it with intelligence. It is not to me a vital matter, for instance, if three dozen glasses of jelly sit on a kitchen table a day or two after they are prepared for retirement to the fruit cellar. I rather like to see them, marshaled in their neat rows, capped with sealing wax and paper, and armed with labels. But

Maggie has neither sentiment nor imagination. Jelly to her is an institution, not an inspiration. It is subject to certain rules and rites, of which not the least is the formal interment in the fruit closet.

Therefore, after much protesting that night, I agreed to visit the fruit cellar, and select a spot for the temporary entombing of thirty-six jelly tumblers, which would have been thirty-seven had Delia known the efficacy of a silver spoon. I can recall vividly the mental shift from the confession to that domestic excursion, my own impatience, Maggie's grim determination, and the curious *dénouement* of that visit.

CHAPTER III

I HAD THE VERY SLIGHTEST ACQUAINTANCE with the basement of the Benton house. I knew it was dry and orderly, and with that my interest: in it ceased. It was not cemented, but its hard clay floor was almost as solid as macadam. In one end was built a high potato-bin. In another corner two or three old pews from the church, evidently long discarded and showing weather-stains, as though they had once served as garden benches, were up-ended against the whitewashed wall. The fruit-closet, built in of lumber, occupied one entire end, and was virtually a room, with a door and no windows.

Maggie had, she said, found it locked and had had an itinerant locksmith fit a key to it.

"It's all scrubbed and ready," she said. "I found that preserved melon-rind you had for lunch in a corner. 'Twouldn't of kept much longer, so I took it up and opened it. She's probably got all sorts of stuff spoiling in the locked part. Some folks're like that."

Most of the shelves were open, but now, holding the lamp high, I saw that a closet with a door occupied one end. The door was padlocked. At the time I was interested, but I was, as I remember, much more occupied with Maggie's sense of *meum* and *tuum*, which I considered deficient, and of a small lecture on other people's melon rinds, which I delivered as she sullenly put away the jelly.

But that night, after I had gone to bed, the memory of that padlock became strangely insistent. There was nothing psychic about the feeling I had. It was perfectly obvious and simple. The house held, or had held, a secret. Yet it was, above stairs, as open as the day. There was no corner into which I might not peer, except— Why was that portion of the fruit-closet locked?

At two o'clock, finding myself unable to sleep, I got up and put on my dressing-gown and slippers. I had refused to repeat the experiment of being locked in. Then, with a candle and a box of matches, I went downstairs. I had, as I have said, no longer any terror of the lower floor. The cat lay as usual on the table in the back hall. I saw his eyes watching me with their curious unblinking stare, as intelligent as two brass buttons. He rose as my light approached, and I made a bed for him of a cushion from a chair, failing my Paisley shawl.

It was after that that I had the curious sense of being led. It was as though I knew that something awaited my discovery, and that my sole volition was whether I should make that discovery or not. It was there, waiting.

I have no explanation for this. And it is quite possible that I might have had it, to find at the end nothing more significant than root-beer, for instance, or bulbs for the winter garden.

And indeed, at first sight, what awaited me in the locked closet amounted to anti-climax. For when I had broken the rusty padlock open with a hatchet, and had opened doors with nervous fingers, nothing more startling appeared than a number of books. The shelves were piled high with them, a motley crew of all colors, but dark shades predominating.

I went back to bed, sheepishly enough, and wrapped my chilled feet in an extra blanket. Maggie came to the door about the time I was dozing off and said she had heard hammering downstairs in the cellar some time ago, but she had refused to waken me until the burglars had gone.

"If it *was* burglars," she added, "you're that up-and-ready, Miss Agnes, that I knew if I waked you you'd be downstairs after them. What's a bit of silver to a human life?"

I got her away at last, and she went, muttering something about digging up the cellar floor and finding an uneasy spirit. Then I fell asleep.

I had taken cold that night, and the following morning I spent in bed. At noon Maggie came upstairs, holding at arm's length a book. She kept her face averted, and gave me a slanting and outraged glance.

"This is a nice place we've come to," she said, acidly. "Murder in the telephone and anti-Christ in the fruit cellar!"

"Why, Maggie," I expostulated.

"If these books stay, I go, and that's flat, Miss Agnes," was her *ipse dixit*. She dropped the book on the bed and stalked out, pausing at the door only to throw back, "If this is a clergyman's house, I guess I'd be better out of the church."

I took up the book. It was well-worn, and in the front, in a heavy masculine hand, the owner had written his name—written it large, a bit defiantly, perhaps. It had taken both courage and conviction to bring such a book into that devout household.

I am not quick, mentally, especially when it

comes to logical thought. I daresay I am intuitive rather than logical. It was not by any process of reasoning at all, I fancy, that it suddenly seemed strange that there should be books locked away in the cellar. Yet it was strange. For that had been a bookish household. Books were its stock in trade, one may say. Such as I had borrowed from the library had been carefully tended. Torn leaves were neatly repaired. The reference books were alphabetically arranged. And, looking back on my visit to the cellar, I recalled now as inconsistent the disorder of those basement shelves.

I did not reach the truth until, that afternoon, I made a second visit to the cellar. Mrs. Graves had been mistaken. If not all Carlo Benton's proscribed books were hidden there, at least a large portion of his library was piled, in something like confusion, on the shelves. Yet she maintained that they had searched the house, and she herself had been present when the books were packed and taken away to the river.

That afternoon I returned Mrs. Graves's visit. She was at home, and in a sort of flurried neatness that convinced me she had seen me from far up the road. That conviction was increased by the amazing promptness with which a tea-tray followed my entrance. I had given her tea the day she came to see me, and she was not to be outdone. Indeed, I somehow gained the impression that tray and teapot, and even little cakes, had been waiting, day by day, for my anticipated visit.

It was not hard to set her talking of Carlo Benton and his wickedness. She rose to the bait like a hungry fish. Yet I gathered that, beyond his religious views or lack of them, she knew nothing. But on the matter of the books she was firm.

"After the box was ready," she said, "we went to every room and searched it. Miss Emily was set on clearing out every trace. At the last minute I found one called *The Fallacy of Christianity* slipped down behind the dresser in his room, and we put that in."

It was *The Fallacy of Christianity* that Maggie had brought me that morning.

"It is a most interesting story," I observed. "What delicious tea, Mrs. Graves! And then you fastened up the box and saw it thrown into the river. It was quite a ceremony."

"My dear," Mrs. Graves said solemnly, "it was not a ceremony. It was a rite—a significant rite."

How can I reconcile the thoughts I had that afternoon with my later visit to Miss Emily? The little upper room in the village, dominated and almost filled by an old-fashioned bed, and Miss Emily, frail and delicate and beautifully neat, propped with pillows and holding a fine handkerchief, as fresh as the flutings of her small cap, in her hand. On a small stand beside the bed were her Bible, her spectacles, and her quaint old-fashioned gold watch.

And Miss Emily herself? She was altered, shockingly altered. A certain tenseness had gone, a tenseness that had seemed to uphold her frail body and carry her about. Only her eyes seemed greatly alive, and before I left they, too, had ceased their searching of mine and looked weary and old.

And, at the end of my short visit, I had reluctantly reached this conclusion: either Miss Emily had done the thing she confessed to doing, incredible as it might appear, or she thought she had done it; and the thing was killing her.

She knew I had found the confession. I knew that. It was written large over her. What she had expected me to do God only knows. To stand up and denounce her? To summon the law? I do not know.

She said an extraordinary thing, when at last I rose to go. I believe now that it was to give me my chance to speak. Probably she found the suspense intolerable. But I could not do it. I was too surprised, too perplexed, too—well, afraid of hurting her. I had the feeling, I know, that I must protect her. And that feeling never left me until the end.

"I think you must know, my dear," she said, from her pillows, "that I have your Paisley shawl."

I was breathless. "I thought that, perhaps—" I stumbled.

"It was raining that night," she said in her soft, delicate voice. "I have had it dried and pressed. It is not hurt. I thought you would not mind," she concluded.

"It does not matter at all—not in the least," I said unhappily.

I am quite sure now that she meant me to speak then. I can recall the way she fixed her eyes on me, serene and expectant. She was waiting. But to save my life I could not. And she did not. Had she gone as far as she had the strength to go? Or was this again one of those curious pacts of hers— if I spoke or was silent, it was to be?

I do not know.

I do know that we were both silent and that at last, with a quick breath, she reached out and thumped on the floor with a cane that stood beside the bed until a girl came running up from below stairs.

"Get the shawl, Fanny, dear," said Miss Emily, "and wrap it up for Miss Blakiston."

I wanted desperately, while the girl left the room to obey, to say something helpful, something reassuring. But I could not. My voice failed me. And Miss Emily did not give me another opportunity. She thanked me rather formally for the flowers I had brought from her garden, and let me go at last with the parcel under my arm, without further reference to it. The situation was incredible.

Somehow I had the feeling that Miss Emily would never reopen the subject again. She had given me my chance, at who knows what cost, and I had not taken it. There had been something in her good-by—I can not find words for it, but it was perhaps a finality, an effect of a closed door— that I felt without being able to analyze.

I walked back to the house, refusing the offices of Mr. Staley, who met me on the road. I needed to think. But thinking took me nowhere. Only one conclusion stood out as a result of a mile and a half of mental struggle. Something must be done. Miss Emily ought to be helped. She was under a strain that was killing her.

But to help I should know the facts. Only, were there any facts to know? Suppose—just by way of argument, for I did not believe it—that the confession was true; how could I find out anything about it? Five years was a long time. I could not go to the neighbors. They were none too friendly as it was. Besides, the secret, if there was one, was not mine, but was Miss Emily's.

I reached home at last, and smuggled the shawl into the house. I had no intention of explaining its return to Maggie. Yet, small as it was in its way, it offered a problem at once. For Maggie has a penetrating eye and an inquiring nature. I finally decided to take the bull by the horns and hang it in its accustomed place in the hail, where Maggie, finding it at nine o'clock that evening, set up such a series of shrieks and exclamations as surpassed even her own record.

I knitted that evening. It has been my custom for years to knit bedroom-slippers for an old ladies' home in which I am interested. Because I can work at them with my eyes shut, through long practise, I find the work soothing. So that evening I knitted at Eliza Klinordlinger's fifth annual right slipper, and tried to develop a course of action.

I began with a major premise—to regard the confession as a real one, until it was proved otherwise. Granted, then, that my little old Miss Emily had killed a woman.

1st—Who was the woman?

2nd—Where is the body?

3rd—What was the reason for the crime?

Question two I had a tentative answer for. However horrible and incredible it seemed, it was at least possible that Miss Emily had substituted the body for the books, and that what Mrs. Graves described as a rite had indeed been one. But that brought up a picture I could not face.

And yet—

I called up the local physician, a Doctor Lingard, that night and asked him about Miss Emily's condition. He was quite frank with me.

"It's just a breaking up," he said. "It has come early, because she has had a trying life, and more responsibility than she should have had."

"I have been wondering if a change of scene would not be a good thing," I suggested. But he was almost scornful.

"Change!" he said. "I've been after her to get away for years. She won't leave. I don't believe she has been twelve miles away in thirty years."

"I suppose her brother was a great care," I observed.

It seemed to me that the doctor's hearty voice was a trifle less frank when he replied. But when I rang off I told myself that I, too, was becoming neurasthenic and suspicious. I had, however, learned what I had wanted to know. Miss Emily had had no life outside Bolivar County. The place to look for her story was here, in the immediate vicinity.

That night I made a second visit to the basement. It seemed to me, with those chaotic shelves before me, that something of the haste and terror of a night five years before came back to me, a night when, confronted by the necessity for concealing a crime, the box upstairs had been hurriedly unpacked, its contents hidden here and locked away, and some other content, inert and heavy, had taken the place of the books.

Miss Emily in her high bed, her Bible and spectacles on the stand beside her, her starched pillows, her soft and highbred voice? Or another Miss Emily, panting and terror-stricken, carrying down her armfuls of forbidden books, her slight figure bent under their weight, her ears open for sounds from the silent house? Or that third Miss Emily, Martin Sprague's, a strange wild creature, neither sane nor insane, building a crime out of the fabric of a nightmare? Which was the real Emily Benton?

Or was there another contingency that I had not thought of? Had some secret enemy of Miss Emily's, some hysterical girl from the parish, suffering under a fancied slight, or some dismissed and revengeful servant, taken this strange method of retaliation, done it and then warned the little old lady that her house contained such a paper? I confess that this last thought took hold on me. It offered a way out that I clutched at.

I had an almost frantic feeling by that time that I must know the truth. Suspense was weighing on me. And Maggie, never slow to voice an unpleasant truth, said that night, as she brought the carafe of ice-water to the library, "You're going off the last few days, Miss Agnes." And when I made no reply: "You're sagging around the chin. There's nothing shows age like the chin. If you'd rub a little lemon-juice on at night you'd tighten up some."

I ignored her elaborately, but I knew she was right. Heat and sleepless nights and those early days of fear had told on me. And although I usually disregard Maggie's cosmetic suggestions, culled from the beauty columns of the evening paper, a look in the mirror decided me. I went downstairs for the lemon. At least, I thought it was for the lemon. I am not sure. I have come to be uncertain of my motives. It is distinctly possible that, sub-consciously, I was making for the cellar all the time. I only know that I landed there, with a lemon in my hand, at something after eleven o'clock.

The books were piled in disorder on the shelves. Their five years of burial had not hurt them beyond a slight dampness of the leaves. No hand, I believe, had touched them since they were taken from the box where Mrs. Graves had helped to pack them. Then, if I were shrewd, I should perhaps gather something from their very disorder. But, as a matter of fact, I did not.

I would, quite certainly, have gone away as I came, clueless, had I not attempted to straighten a pile of books, dangerously sagging—like my chin!—and threatening a fall. My effort was rewarded by a veritable Niagara of books. They poured over the edge, a few first, then more, until I stood, it seemed, knee-deep in a raging sea of atheism.

Somewhat grimly I set to work to repair the damage, and one by one I picked them up and restored them. I put them in methodically this time, glancing at each title to place the volume upright. Suddenly, out of the darkness of unbelief, a title caught my eye and held it, *The Handwriting of God*. I knew the book. It had fallen into bad company, but its theology was unimpeachable. It did not belong. It—

I opened it. The Reverend Samuel Thaddeus had written his own name in it, in the cramped hand I had grown to know. Evidently its presence there was accidental. I turned it over in my hands, and saw that it was closed down on something, on several things, indeed. They proved to be a small black notebook, a pair of spectacles, a woman's handkerchief.

I stood there looking at them. They might mean nothing but the accidental closing of a book, which was mistakenly placed in bad company, perhaps by Mrs. Graves. I was inclined to doubt her knowledge of religious literature. Or they might mean something more, something I had feared to find.

Armed with the volume, and the lemon forgotten—where the cook found it the next day and made much of the mystery—I went upstairs again.

Viewed in a strong light, the three articles took on real significance. The spectacles I fancied were Miss Emily's. They were, to all appearances, the duplicates of those on her tidy bedside stand. But the handkerchief was not hers. Even without the scent, which had left it, but clung obstinately to the pages of the book, I knew it was not hers. It was florid, embroidered, and cheap. And held close to the light, I made out a laundry-mark in ink on the border. The name was either Wright or Knight.

The notebook was an old one, and covered a period of almost twenty years. It contained dates and cash entries. The entries were nearly all in the Reverend Samuel Thaddeus's hand, but after the date of his death they had been continued in Miss Emily's writing. They varied little, save that the amounts gradually increased toward the end, and the dates were further apart. Thus, in 1898 there were six entries, aggregating five hundred dollars. In 1902-1903 there were no entries at all, but in 1904 there was a single memorandum of a thousand dollars. The entire amount must have been close to twenty-five thousand dollars. There was nothing to show whether it was money saved or money spent, money paid out or come in.

But across the years 1902 and 1903, the Reverend Thaddeus had written diagonally the word "Australia." There was a certain amount of enlightenment there. Carlo Benton had been in Australia during those years. In his *Fifty Years in Bolivar County*, the father had rather naively quoted a letter from Carlo Benton in Melbourne. A record, then, in all probability, of sums paid by this harassed old man to a worthless son.

Only the handkerchief refused to be accounted for.

I did not sleep that night. More and more, as I lay wide-eyed through the night, it seemed to me that Miss Emily must be helped, that she was drifting miserably out of life for need of a helping hand.

Once, toward morning, I dozed off, to waken in a state of terror that I recognized as a return of the old fear. But it left me soon, although I lay awake until morning.

That day I made two resolves—to send for Willie and to make a determined effort to see the night telephone-operator. My letter to Willie off, I tried to fill the day until the hour when the night telephone-operator was up and about, late in the afternoon.

The delay was simplified by the arrival of Mrs. Graves, in white silk gloves and a black cotton umbrella as a sunshade. She had lost her air of being afraid I might patronize her, and explained pantingly that she had come on an errand, not to call.

"I'm at my Christmas presents now," she said, "and I've fixed on a bedroom set for Miss Emily. I suppose you won't care if I go right up and measure the dresser-top, will you?"

I took her up, and her sharp eyes roved over the stairs and the upper hall.

"That's where Carlo died," she said. "It's never been used since, unless you—" she had paused, staring into Miss Emily's deserted bedroom. "It's a good thing I came," she said. "The eye's no use to trust to, especially for bureaus."

She looked around the room. There was, at that moment, something tender about her. She even lowered her voice and softened it. It took on, almost comically, the refinements of Miss Emily's own speech.

"Whose photograph is that?" she asked suddenly. "I don't know that I ever saw it before. But it looks familiar, too."

She reflected before it. It was clear that she felt a sort of resentment at not recognizing the young and smiling woman in the old walnut frame, but a moment later she was measuring the dressertop, her mind set on Christmas benevolence.

However, before she went out, she paused near the photograph.

"It's queer," she said. "I've been in this room about a thousand times, and I've never noticed it before. I suppose you can get so accustomed to a thing that you don't notice it."

As she went out, she turned to me, and I gathered that not only the measurement for a gift had brought her that afternoon.

"About those books," she said. "I run on a lot when I get to talking. I suppose I shouldn't have mentioned them. But I'm sure you'll keep the story to yourself. I've never even told Mr. Graves."

"Of course I shall," I assured her. "But—didn't

the hackman see you packing the books?"

"No, indeed. We packed them the afternoon after the funeral, and it was the next day that Staley took them off. He thought it was old bedding and so on, and he hinted to have it given to him. So Miss Emily and I went along to see it was done right."

So I discovered that the box had sat overnight in the Benton house.

There remained, if I was to help Miss Emily, to discover what had occurred in those dark hours when the books were taken out and something else substituted.

The total result of my conversation that afternoon on the front porch of the small frame house on a side street with the night telephone-operator was additional mystery.

I was not prepared for it. I had anticipated resentment and possibly insolence. But I had not expected to find fright. Yet the girl was undeniably frightened. I had hardly told her the object of my visit before I realized that she was in a state of almost panic.

"You can understand how I feel," I said. "I have no desire to report the matter, of course. But some one has been calling the house repeatedly at night, listening until I reply, and then hanging up the receiver. It is not accidental. It has happened too often."

"I'm not supposed to give out information about calls."

"But—just think a moment," I went on. "Suppose some one is planning to rob the house, and using this method of finding out if we arc there or not?"

"I don't remember anything about the calls you are talking about," she parried, without looking at me. "As busy as I am—"

"Nonsense," I put in, "you know perfectly well what I am talking about. How do I know but that it is the intention of some one to lure me downstairs to the telephone and then murder me?"

"I am sure it is not that," she said. For almost the first time she looked directly at me, and I caught a flash of something—not defiance. It was, indeed, rather like reassurance.

"You see, you *know* it is not that." I felt all at once that she did know who was calling me at night, and why. And, moreover, that she would not tell. If, as I suspected, it was Miss Emily, this girl must be to some extent in her confidence.

"But—suppose for a moment that I think I know who is calling me?" I hesitated. She was a pretty girl, with an amiable face, and more than a suggestion of good breeding and intelligence about her. I made a quick resolve to appeal to her. "My dear child," I said, "I want so very much, if I can, to help some one who is in trouble. But before I can help, I must know that I can help, and I must be sure it is necessary. I wonder if you know what I am talking about?"

"Why don't you go back to the city?" she said suddenly. "Go away and forget all about us here. That would help more than anything."

"But—would it?" I asked gently. "Would my going away help her?"

To my absolute amazement she began to cry. We had been sitting on a cheap porch seat, side by side, and she turned her back to me and put her head against the arm of the bench.

"She's going to die!" she said shakily. "She's weaker every day. She is slipping away, and no one does anything."

But I got nothing more from her. She had understood me, it was clear, and when at last she stopped crying, she knew well enough that she had betrayed her understanding. But she would not talk. I felt that she was not unfriendly, and that she was uncertain rather than stubborn. In the end I got up, little better off than when I came.

"I'll give you time to think it over," I said. "Not so much about the telephone calls, because you've really answered that. But about Miss Emily. She needs help, and I want to help her. But you tie my hands."

She had a sort of gift for silence. As I grew later on to know Anne Bullard better, I realized that even more. So now she sat silent, and let me talk.

"What I want," I said, "is to have Miss Emily know that I am friendly—that I am willing to do anything to—to show my friendliness. *Anything.*"

"You see," she said, with a kind of dogged patience, "it isn't really up to you, or to me either. It's something else." She hesitated. "She's very obstinate," she added.

When I went away I was aware that her eyes followed me, anxious and thoughtful eyes, with something of Miss Emily's own wide-eyed gaze.

Willie came late the next evening. I had indeed gone upstairs to retire when I heard his car in the drive. When I admitted him, he drew me into the library and gave me a good looking over.

"As I thought!" he said. "Nerves gone, looks gone. I told you Maggie would put a curse on you. What is it?"

So I told him. The telephone he already knew about. The confession he read over twice, and then observed, characteristically, that he would be eternally—I think the word is "hornswoggled."

When I brought out *The Handwriting of God,* following Mrs. Graves's story of the books, he looked thoughtful. And indeed by the end of the recital he was very grave.

"Sprague is a lunatic," he said, with conviction. "There was a body, and it went into the river in the packing-case. It is distinctly possible that this

Knight—or Wright—woman, who owned the handkerchief, was the victim. However, that's for later on. The plain truth is, that there was a murder, and that Miss Emily is shielding some one else."

And, after all, that was the only immediate result of Willie's visit—a new theory! So that now it stood: there was a crime. There was no crime. Miss Emily had committed it. Miss Emily had not committed it. Miss Emily had confessed it, but some one else had committed it.

For a few hours, however, our attention was distracted from Miss Emily and her concerns by the attempted robbery of the house that night. I knew nothing of it until I heard Willie shouting downstairs. I was deeply asleep, relaxed no doubt by the consciousness that at last there was a man in the house. And, indeed, Maggie slept for the same reason through the entire occurrence.

"Stop, or I'll fire!" Willie repeated, as I sat up in bed.

I knew quite well that he had no weapon. There was not one in the house. But the next moment there was a loud report, either a door slamming or a pistol shot, and I ran to the head of the stairs.

There was no light below, but a current of cool night air came up the staircase. And suddenly I realized that there was complete silence in the house.

"Willie!" I cried out, in an agony of fright. But he did not reply. And then, suddenly, the telephone rang.

I did not answer it. I know now why it rang, that there was real anxiety behind its summons. But I hardly heard it then. I was convinced that Willie had been shot.

I must have gone noiselessly down the stairs, and at the foot I ran directly into Willie. He was standing there, only a deeper shadow in the blackness, and I had placed my hand over his, as it lay on the newel-post, before he knew I was on the staircase. He wheeled sharply, and I felt, to my surprise, that he held a revolver in his hand.

"Willie! What is it?" I said in a low tone.

"Sh," he whispered. "Don't move—or speak."

We listened, standing together. There were undoubtedly sounds outside, some one moving about, a hand on a window-catch, and finally not particularly cautious steps at the front door. It swung open. I could hear it creak as it moved slowly on its hinges.

I put a hand out to steady myself by the comfort of Willie's presence before me, between me and that softly-opening door. But Willie was moving forward, crouched down, I fancied, and the memory of that revolver terrified me.

"Don't shoot him, Willie!" I almost shrieked.

"Shoot whom?" said Willie's cool voice, just inside the door.

I knew then, and I went sick all over. Somewhere in the hall between us crouched the man I had taken for Willie, crouched with a revolver in his right hand. The door was still open, I knew, and I could hear Willie fumbling on the hall-stand for matches. I called out something incoherent about not striking a light; but Willie, whistling softly to show how cool he was, struck a match. It was followed instantly by a report, and I closed my eyes.

When I opened them, Willie was standing unhurt, staring over the burning match at the door, which was closed, and I knew that the report had been but the bang of the heavy door.

"What in blazes slammed that door?" he said.

"The burglar, or whatever he is," I said, my voice trembling in spite of me. "He was here, in front of me. I laid my hand on his. He had a revolver in it. When you opened the door, he slipped out past you."

Willie muttered something, and went toward the door. A moment later I was alone again, and the telephone was ringing. I felt my way back along the hall. I touched the cat, which had been sleeping on the telephone-stand. He merely turned over.

I have tried, in living that night over again, to record things as they impressed me. For, after all, this is a narrative of motive rather than of incidents, of emotions as against deeds. But at the time, the brief conversation over the telephone seemed to me both horrible and unnatural.

From a great distance a woman's voice said, "Is anything wrong there?"

That was the first question, and I felt quite sure that it was the Bullard girl's voice. That is, looking back from the safety of the next day, I so decided. At the time I had no thought whatever.

"There is nothing wrong," I replied. I do not know why I said it. Surely there was enough wrong, with Willie chasing an armed intruder through the garden.

I thought the connection had been cut, for there was a buzzing on the wire. But a second or so later there came an entirely different voice, one I had never heard before, a plaintive voice, full, I thought, of tears.

"Oh, please," said this voice, "go out and look in your garden, or along the road. Please—quickly!"

"You will have to explain," I said impatiently. "Of course we will go and look, but who is it, and why—"

I was cut off there, definitely, and I could not get "Central's" attention again.

Willie's voice from the veranda boomed through the lower floor. "This is I," he called, "No boiling water, please. I am coming in."

He went into the library and lighted a lamp. He

was smiling when I entered, a reassuring smile, but rather a sheepish one, too.

"To think of letting him get by like that!" he said. "The cheapest kind of a trick. He had slammed the door before to make me think he had gone out, and all the time he was inside. And you—why didn't you scream?"

"I thought it was you," I told him.

The library was in chaos. Letters were lying about, papers, books. The drawer of the large desk-table in the center of the room had been drawn out and searched. *Fifty Years in Bolivar County*, for instance, was lying on the floor, face down, in a most ignoble position. In one place books had been taken from a recess by the fireplace, revealing a small wall cupboard behind. I had never known of the hiding-place, but a glance into it revealed only a bottle of red ink and the manuscript of a sermon on missions.

Standing in the disorder of the room, I told Willie about the telephone message. He listened attentively, and at first skeptically.

"Probably a ruse to get us out of the house, but coming a trifle late to be useful," was his comment. But I had read distress in the second voice, and said so. At last he went to the telephone.

"I'll verify it," he explained. "If some one is really anxious, I'll get the car and take a scout around."

But he received no satisfaction from the Bullard girl, who, he reported, listened stoically and then said she was sorry, but she did not remember who had called. On his reminding her that she must have a record, she countered with the flat statement that there had been no call for us that night.

Willie looked thoughtful when he returned to the library. "There's a queer story back of all this," he said. "I think I'll get the car and scout around."

"He is armed, Willie," I protested.

"He doesn't want to shoot me, or he could have done it," was his answer. "I'll just take a look around, and come back to report."

It was half-past three by the time he was ready to go. He was, as he observed, rather sketchily clad, but the night was warm. I saw him off, and locked the door behind him. Then I went into the library to wait and to put things to rights while I waited.

The dawn is early in August, and although it was not more than half-past four when Willie came back, it was about daylight by that time. I went to the door and watched him bring the car to a standstill. He shook his head when he saw me.

"Absolutely nothing," he said. "It was a ruse to get me out of the house, of course. I've run the whole way between here and town twice."

"But that could not have taken an hour," I

protested.

"No," he said. "I met the doctor—what's his name?—the local M.D. anyhow—footing it out of the village to a case, and I took him to his destination. He has a car, it seems, but it's out of order. Interesting old chap," he added, as I led the way into the house. "Didn't know me from Adam, but opened up when he found who I was."

I had prepared the coffee machine and carried the tray to the library. While I lighted the lamp, he stood, whistling softly, and thoughtfully. At last he said:

"Look here, Aunt Agnes, I think I'm a good bit of a fool, but some time this morning I wish you would call up Thomas Jenkins, on the Elmburg road, and find out if any one is sick there."

But when I stared at him, he only laughed sheepishly. "You can see how your suspicious disposition has undermined and ruined my once trusting nature," he scoffed.

He took his coffee, and then, stripping off his ulster, departed for bed. I stopped to put away the coffee machine, and with Maggie in mind, to hang up his coat. It was then that the flashlight fell out. I picked it up. It was shaped like a revolver.

I stopped in Willie's room on my way to my own, and held it out to him.

"Where did you get that?" I asked.

"Good heavens!" he said, raising himself on his

elbow. "It belongs to the doctor. He gave it to me to examine the fan belt. I must have dropped it into my pocket."

And still I was nowhere. Suppose I had touched this flashlight at the foot of the stairs and mistaken it for a revolver. Suppose that the doctor, making his way toward the village and finding himself pursued, had faced about and pretended to be leaving it? Grant, in a word, that Doctor Lingard himself had been our night visitor what then? Why had he done it? What of the telephone-call, urging me to search the road? Did some one realize what was happening, and take this method of warning us and sending us after the fugitive?

I knew the Thomas Jenkins farm on the Elmsburg road. I had, indeed, bought vegetables and eggs from Mr. Jenkins himself. That morning, as early as I dared, I called the Jenkins farm. Mr. Jenkins himself would bring me three dozen eggs that day. They were a little torn up out there, as Mrs. Jenkins had borne a small daughter at seven A.M.

When I told Willie, he was evidently relieved. "I'm glad of it," he said heartily. "The doctor's a fine old chap, and I'd hate to think he was mixed up in any shady business."

He was insistent, that day, that I give up the house. He said it was not safe, and I was inclined to agree with him. But although I did not tell him of it, I had even more strongly than ever the impression that something must be done to help Miss Emily, and that I was the one who must do it.

Yet, in the broad light of day, with the sunshine pouring into the rooms, I was compelled to confess that Willie's theory was more than upheld by the facts. First of all was the character of Miss Emily as I read it, sternly conscientious, proud, and yet gentle. Second, there was the connection of the Bullard girl with the case. And third, there was the invader of the night before, an unknown quantity where so much seemed known, where a situation involving Miss Emily alone seemed to call for no one else.

Willie put the matter flatly to me as he stood in the hall, drawing on his driving gloves.

"Do you *want* to follow it up?" he asked. "Isn't it better to let it go? After all, you have only rented the house. You haven't taken over its history, or any responsibility but the rent."

"I think Miss Emily needs to be helped," I said, rather feebly.

"Let her friends help her. She has plenty of them. Besides, isn't it rather a queer way to help her, to try to fasten a murder on her?"

I could not explain what I felt so strongly—that Miss Emily could only be helped by being hurt, that whatever she was concealing, the long concealment was killing her. That I felt in her—it is always difficult to put what I felt about Miss Emily into words—that she both hoped for and dreaded desperately the light of the truth.

But if I was hardly practical when it came to Miss Emily, I was rational enough in other things. It is with no small pride—but without exultation, for in the end it cost too much—that I point to the solution of one issue as my own.

With Willie gone, Maggie and I settled down to the quiet tenure of our days. She informed me, on the morning after that eventful night, that she had not closed an eye after one o'clock! She came into the library and asked me if I could order her some sleeping-powders.

"Fiddlesticks!" I said sharply. "You slept all night. I was up and around the house, and you never knew it."

"Honest to heaven, Miss Agnes, I never slep' at all. I heard a horse gallopin', like it was runnin' off, and it waked me for good."

And after a time I felt that, however mistaken Maggie had been about her night's sleep, she was possibly correct about the horse.

"He started to run about the stable somewhere," she said. "You can smile if you want. That's the heaven's truth. And he came down the drive on the jump and out onto the road."

"We can go and look for hoof-marks," I said, and rose. But Maggie only shook her head.

"It was no real horse, Miss Agnes," she said. "You'll find nothing. Anyhow, I've been and looked. There's not a mark."

But Maggie was wrong. I found hoof-prints in plenty in the turf beside the drive, and a track of them through the lettuce-bed in the garden. More than that, behind the stable I found where a horse had been tied and had broken away. A piece of worn strap still hung there. It was sufficiently clear, then, that whoever had broken into the house had come on horseback and left afoot. But many people in the neighborhood used horses. The clue, if clue it can be called, got me nowhere.

CHAPTER IV

FOR SEVERAL DAYS THINGS REMAINED in *statu quo.* Our lives went on evenly. The telephone was at our service, without any of its past vagaries. Maggie's eyes ceased to look as if they were being pushed out from behind, and I ceased to waken at night and listen for untoward signs.

Willie telephoned daily. He was frankly uneasy about my remaining there. "You know something that somebody resents your knowing," he said, a day or two after the night visitor. "It may become very uncomfortable for you."

And, after a day or two, I began to feel that it

was being made uncomfortable for me. I am a social being; I like people. In the city my neighborly instincts have died of a sort of brick wall apathy, but in the country it comes to life again. The instinct of gregariousness is as old as the first hamlets, I daresay, when prehistoric man ceased to live in trees, and banded together for protection from the wild beasts that walked the earth.

The village became unfriendly. It was almost a matter of a night. One day the postmistress leaned on the shelf at her window and chatted with me. The next she passed out my letters with hardly a glance. Mrs. Graves did not see me at early communion on Sunday morning. The hackman was busy when I called him. It was intangible, a matter of omission, not commission. The doctor's wife, who had asked me to tea, called up and regretted that she must go to the city that day.

I sat down then and took stock of things. Did the village believe that Miss Emily must be saved from me? Did the village know the story I was trying to learn, and was it determined I should never find out the truth? And, if this were so, was the village right or was I? They would save Miss Emily by concealment, while I felt that concealment had failed, and that only the truth would do. Did the village know, or only suspect? Or was it not the village at all, but one or two people who were determined to drive me away?

My theories were rudely disturbed shortly after that by a visit from Martin Sprague. I fancied that Willie had sent him, but he evaded my question.

"I'd like another look at that slip of paper," he said. "Where do you keep it, by the way?"

"In a safe place," I replied noncommittally, and he laughed. The truth was that I had taken out the removable inner sole of a slipper and had placed it underneath, an excellent hiding-place, but one I did not care to confide to him. When I had brought it downstairs, he read it over again carefully, and then sat back with it in his hand.

"Now tell me about everything," he said.

I did, while he listened attentively. Afterward we walked back to the barn, and I showed him the piece of broken halter still tied there.

He surveyed it without comment, but on the way back to the house he said: "If the village is lined up as you say it is, I suppose it is useless to interview the harness-maker. He has probably repaired that strap, or sold a new one, to whoever—It would be a nice clue to follow up."

"I am not doing detective work," I said shortly. "I am trying to help some one who is dying of anxiety and terror."

He nodded. "I get you," he said. But his tone was not flippant. "The fact is, of course, that the early theory won't hold. There has been a crime, and the little old lady did not commit it. But suppose you find out who did it. How is that going to help her?"

"I don't know, Martin," I said, in a sort of desperation. "But I have the most curious feeling that she is depending on me. The way she spoke the day I saw her, and her eyes and everything; I know you think it nonsense," I finished lamely.

"I think you'd better give up the place and go back to town," he said. But I saw that he watched me carefully, and when, at last he got up to go, he put a hand on my shoulder.

"I think you are right, after all," he said. "There are a good many things that can't be reasoned out with any logic we have, but that are true, nevertheless. We call it intuition, but it's really subconscious intelligence. Stay, by all means, if you feel you should."

In the doorway he said: "Remember this, Miss Agnes. Both a crime of violence and a confession like the one in your hand are the products of impulse. They are not, either of them, premeditated. They are not the work, then, of a calculating or cautious nature. Look for a big, emotional type."

It was a day or two after that that I made my visit to Miss Emily. I had stopped once before, to be told with an air of finality that the invalid was asleep. On this occasion I took with me a basket of fruit. I had half expected a refusal, but I was admitted.

The Bullard girl was with Miss Emily. She had, I think, been kneeling beside the bed, and her eyes were red and swollen. But Miss Emily herself was as cool, as dainty and starched and fragile as ever. More so, I thought. She was thinner, and although it was a warm August day, a white silk shawl was wrapped around her shoulders and fastened with an amethyst brooch. In my clasp her thin hand felt hot and dry.

"I have been waiting for you," she said simply.

She looked at Anne Bullard, and the message in her eyes was plain enough. But the girl ignored it. She stood across the bed from me and eyed me steadily.

"My dear," said Miss Emily, in her high-bred voice, "if you have anything to do, Miss Blakiston will sit with me for a little while."

"I have nothing to do," said the girl doggedly. Perhaps this is not the word. She had more the look of endurance and supreme patience. There was no sharpness about her, although there was vigilance.

Miss Emily sighed, and I saw her eyes seek the Bible beside her. But she only said gently: "Then sit down, dear. You can work at my knitting if you like. My hands get very tired."

She asked me questions about the house and the garden. The raspberries were usually quite good, and she was rather celebrated for her lettuces. If I had more than I needed, would I mind if Mr. Staley took a few in to the doctor, who was fond of them.

The mention of Doctor Lingard took me back to the night of the burglary. I wondered if to tell Miss Emily would unduly agitate her. I think I would not have told her, but I caught the girl's eye, across the bed, raised from her knitting and fixed on me with a peculiar intensity. Suddenly it seemed to me that Miss Emily was surrounded by a conspiracy of silence, and it roused my antagonism.

"There are plenty of lettuces," I said, "although a few were trampled by a runaway horse the other night. It is rather a curious story."

So I told her of our night visitor. I told it humorously, lightly, touching on my own horror at finding I had been standing with my hand on the burglar's shoulder. But I was sorry for my impulse immediately, for I saw Miss Emily's body grow rigid, and her hands twist together. She did not look at me. She stared fixedly at the girl. Their eyes met.

It was as if Miss Emily asked a question which the girl refused to answer. It was as certain as though it had been a matter of words instead of glances. It was over in a moment. Miss Bullard went back to her knitting, but Miss Emily lay still.

"I think I should not have told you," I

apologized. "I thought it might interest you. Of course nothing whatever was taken, and no damage done—except to the lettuces."

"Anne," said Miss Emily, "will you bring me some fresh water?"

The girl rose reluctantly, but she did not go farther than the top of the staircase, just beyond the door. We heard her calling to some one below, in her clear young voice, to bring the water, and the next moment she was back in the room. But Miss Emily had had the opportunity for one sentence.

"I know now," she said quietly, "that you have found it."

Anne Bullard was watching from the doorway, and it seemed to me, having got so far, I could not retreat. I must go on.

"Miss Bullard," I said. "I would like to have just a short conversation with Miss Emily. It is about a private matter. I am sure you will not mind if I ask you—"

"I shall not go out."

"Anne!" said Miss Emily sharply.

The girl was dogged enough by that time. Both dogged and frightened, I felt. But she stood her ground.

"She is not to be worried about anything," she insisted. "And she's not supposed to have visitors. That's the doctor's orders."

I felt outraged and indignant, but against the

stone wall of the girl's presence and her distrust I was helpless. I got up, with as much dignity as I could muster.

"I should have been told that downstairs."

"The woman's a fool," said Anne Bullard, with a sort of suppressed fierceness. She stood aside as, having said good-by to Miss Emily, I went out, and I felt that she hardly breathed until I had got safely to the street.

Looking back, I feel that Emily Benton died at the hands of her friends. For she died, indeed, died in the act of trying to tell me what they had determined she should never tell. Died of kindness and misunderstanding. Died repressed, as she had lived repressed. Yet, I think, died calmly and bravely.

I had made no further attempt to see her, and Maggie and I had taken up again the quiet course of our lives. The telephone did not ring of nights. The cat came and went, spending as I had learned, its days with Miss Emily and its nights with us. I have wondered since how many nights Miss Emily had spent in the low chair in that back hall, where the confession lay hidden, that the cat should feel it could sleep nowhere else.

The days went by, warm days and cooler ones, but rarely rainy ones. The dust from the road settled thick over flowers and shrubbery. The lettuces wilted, and those that stood up in the sun were strong and bitter. By the end of August we were gasping in a hot dryness that cracked the skin and made any but cold food impossible.

Miss Emily lay through it all in her hot upper room in the village, and my attempt, through Doctor Lingard, to coax her back to the house by offering to leave it brought only a negative.

"It would be better for her, you understand," the doctor said, over the telephone. "But she is very determined, and she insists on remaining where she is."

And I believe this was the truth. They would surely have been glad to get rid of me, these friends of Miss Emily's.

I have wondered since what they thought of me, Anne Bullard and the doctor, to have feared me as they did. I look in the mirror, and I see a middle-aged woman, with a determined nose, slightly inquisitive, and what I trust is a humorous mouth, for it has no other virtues. But they feared me. Perhaps long looking for a danger affects the mental vision. Anyhow, by the doctor's order, I was not allowed to call and see Miss Emily again.

Then, one night, the heat suddenly lifted. One moment I was sitting on the veranda, lifeless and inert, and the next a cool wind, with a hint of rain, had set the shutters to banging and the curtains to flowing, like flags of truce, from the windows. The air was life, energy. I felt revivified.

And something of the same sort must have happened to Miss Emily. She must have sat up among her pillows, her face fanned with the electric breeze, and made her determination to see me. Anne Bullard was at work, and she was free from observation.

It must have been nine o'clock when she left the house, a shaken little figure in black, not as neat as usual, but hooked and buttoned, for all that, with no one will ever know what agony of old hands.

She was two hours and a half getting to the house, and the rain came at ten o'clock. By half after eleven, when the doorbell rang, she was a sodden mass of wet garments, and her teeth were chattering when I led her into the library.

She could not talk. The thing she had come to say was totally beyond her. I put her to bed in her own room. And two days later she died.

I had made no protest when Anne Bullard presented herself at the door the morning after Miss Emily arrived, and, walking into the house, took sleepless charge of the sick room. And I made no reference save once to the reason for the tragedy. That was the night Miss Emily died. Anne Bullard had called to me that she feared there was a change, and I went into the sickroom. There was a change, and I could only shake my head. She burst out at me then.

"If only you had never taken this house!" she said. "You people with money, you think there is nothing you can not have. You came, and now look!"

"Anne," I said with a bitterness I could not conceal, "Miss Emily is not young, and I think she is ready to go. But she has been killed by her friends. I wanted to help, but they would not allow me to."

Toward morning there was nothing more to be done, and we sat together, listening to the stertorous breathing from the bed. Maggie, who had been up all night, had given me notice at three in the morning, and was upstairs packing her trunk.

I went into my room, and brought back Miss Emily's confession.

"Isn't it time," I said, "to tell me about this? I ought to know, I think, before she goes. If it is not true, you owe it to her, I think." But she shook her head.

I looked at the confession, and from it to Miss Emily's pinched old face.

"To whom it may concern: On the 30th day of May, 1911, I killed a woman (here) in this house. I hope you will not find this until I am dead.

(Signed) EMILY BENTON.*"*

Anne was watching me. I went to the mantel and got a match, and then, standing near the bed, I lighted it and touched it to the paper. It burned slowly, a thin blue semicircle of fire that ate its way slowly across until there was but the corner I held. I dropped it into the fireplace and watched it turn to black ash.

I may have fancied it—I am always fancying things about Miss Emily—but I will always think that she knew. She drew a longer, quieter breath, and her eyes, fixed and staring, closed. I think she died in the first sleep she had had in twenty-four hours.

I had expected Anne Bullard to show emotion, for no one could doubt her attachment to Miss Emily. But she only stood stoically by the bed for a moment and then, turning swiftly, went to the wall opposite and took down from the wall the walnut-framed photograph Mrs. Graves had commented on.

Anne Bullard stood with the picture in her hand, looking at it. And suddenly she broke into sobs. It was stormy weeping, and I got the impression that she wept, not for Miss Emily, but for many other things—as though the piled-up grief of years had broken out at last.

She took the photograph away, and I never saw it again.

Miss Emily was buried from her home. I obliterated myself, and her friends, who were, I felt, her murderers, came in and took charge. They paid me the tribute of much politeness, but no cordiality, and I think they felt toward me as I felt toward them. They blamed me with the whole affair.

She left her property all to Anne Bullard, to the astonished rage of the congregation, which had expected the return of its dimes and quarters, no doubt, in the shape of a new altar, or perhaps an organ.

"Not a cent to keep up the mausoleum or anything," Mrs. Graves confided to me. "And nothing to the church. All to that telephone girl, who comes from no one knows where! It's enough to make her father turn over in his grave. It has set people talking, I can tell you."

Maggie's mental state during the days preceding the funeral was curious. She coupled the most meticulous care as to the preparations for the ceremony, and a sort of loving gentleness when she decked Miss Emily's small old frame for its last rites, with suspicion and hatred of Miss Emily living. And this suspicion she held also against Anne Bullard.

Yet she did not want to leave the house. I do not know just what she expected to find. We were cleaning up preparatory to going back to the city, and I felt that at least a part of Maggie's enthusiasm for corners was due to a hope of locating more concealed papers. She was rather less than polite to the Bullard girl, who was staying on at my invitation—because the village was now flagrantly unfriendly and suspicious of her. And for some strange reason, the fact that

Miss Emily's cat followed Anne everywhere convinced Maggie that her suspicions were justified.

"It's like this, Miss Agnes," she said one morning, leaning on the handle of a floor brush. "She had some power over the old lady, and that's how she got the property. And I am saying nothing, but she's no Christian, that girl. To see her and that cat going out night after night, both snooping along on their tiptoes—it ain't normal."

I had several visits from Martin Sprague since Miss Emily's death, and after a time I realized that he was interested in Anne. She was quite attractive in her mourning clothes, and there was something about her, not in feature, but in neatness and in the way her things had of, well, staying in place, that reminded me of Miss Emily herself. It was rather surprising, too, to see the way she fitted into her new surroundings and circumstances.

But I did not approve of Martin's attraction to her. She had volunteered no information about herself, she apparently had no people. She was a lady, I felt, although, with the exception of her new mourning, her clothing was shabby and her linen even coarse.

She held the key to the confession. I knew that. And I had no more hope of getting it from her than I had from the cat. So I prepared to go back to the city, with the mystery unsolved. It seemed a pity, when I had got so far with it. I had reconstructed a situation out of such bricks as I had, the books in the cellar, Mrs. Graves's story of the river, the confession, possibly the notebook and the handkerchief. I had even some material left over in the form of the night intruder, who may or may not have been the doctor. And then, having got so far, I had had to stop for lack of other bricks.

A day or two before I went back to the city, Maggie came to me with a folded handkerchief in her hand.

"Is that yours?" she asked.

I disclaimed it. It was not very fine, and looked rather yellow.

"S'got a name on it," Maggie volunteered. "Wright, I think it is. 'Tain't hers, unless she's picked it up somewhere. It's just come out of the wash."

Maggie's eyes were snapping with suspicion. "There ain't any Wrights around here, Miss Agnes," she said. "I sh'd say she's here under a false name. Wright's likely hers."

In tracing the mystery of the confession, I find that three apparently disconnected discoveries paved the way to its solution. Of these the handkerchief came first.

I was inclined to think that in some manner the handkerchief I had found in the book in the cellar had got into the wash. But it was where I had placed it for safety, in the wall-closet in the library. I brought it out and compared the two. They were unlike, save in the one regard. The name "Wright" was clear enough on the one Maggie had found. With it as a guide, the other name was easily seen to be the same. Moreover, both had been marked by the same hand.

Yet, on Anne Bullard being shown the one Maggie had found, she disclaimed it. "Don't you think some one dropped it at the funeral?" she asked.

But I thought, as I turned away, that she took a step toward me. When I stopped, however, and faced about, she was intent on something outside the window.

And so it went. I got nowhere. And now, by way of complication, I felt my sympathy for Anne's loneliness turning to genuine interest. She was so stoical, so repressed, and so lonely. And she was tremendously proud. Her pride was vaguely reminiscent of Miss Emily's. She bore her ostracism almost fiercely, yet there were times when I felt her eyes on me, singularly gentle and appealing. Yet she volunteered nothing about herself.

I intended to finish the history of Bolivar County before I left. I dislike not finishing a book. Besides, this one fascinated me—the smug complacence and almost loud virtue of the author, his satisfaction in Bolivar County, and his small hits at the world outside, his patronage to those not of it. And always, when I began to read, I turned to the inscription in Miss Emily's hand, the hand of the confession—and I wondered if she had really believed it all.

So on this day I found the name Bullard in the book. It had belonged to the Reverend Samuel Thaddeus's grandmother, and he distinctly stated that she was the last of her line. He inferred, indeed, that since the line was to end, it had chosen a fitting finish in his immediate progenitor.

That night, at dinner, I said, "Anne, are there any Bullards in this neighborhood now?"

"I have never heard of any. But I have not been here long."

"It is not a common name," I persisted.

But she received my statement in silence. She had, as I have said, rather a gift for silence.

That afternoon I was wandering about the garden snipping faded roses with Miss Emily's garden shears, when I saw Maggie coming swiftly toward me. When she caught my eye, she beckoned to me. "Walk quiet, Miss Agnes," she said, "and don't say I didn't warn you. She's in the library."

So, feeling hatefully like a spy, I went quietly over the lawn toward the library windows. They were long ones, to the floor, and at first I made out nothing. Then I saw Anne. She was on her knees, following the border of the carpet with fingers that examined it, inch by inch.

She turned, as if she felt our eyes on her, and saw us. I shall never forget her face. She looked stricken. I turned away. There was something in her eyes that made me think of Miss Emily, lying among her pillows and waiting for me to say the thing she was dreading to hear.

I sent Maggie away with a gesture. There was something in her pursed lips that threatened danger. For I felt then as if I had always known it and only just realized I knew it, that somewhere in that room lay the answer to all questions; lay Miss Emily's secret. And I did not wish to learn it. It was better to go on wondering, to question and doubt and decide and decide again. I was, I think, in a state of nervous terror by that time, terror and apprehension.

While Miss Emily lived, I had hoped to help. But now it seemed too hatefully like accusing when she could not defend herself. And there is another element that I am bound to acknowledge. There was an element of jealousy of Anne Bullard. Both of us had tried to help Miss Emily. She had foiled my attempt in her own endeavor, a mistaken endeavor, I felt. But there was now to be no blemish on my efforts. I would no longer pry or question or watch. It was too late.

In a curious fashion, each of us wished, I think, to prove the quality of her tenderness for the little old lady who was gone beyond all human tenderness.

So that evening, after dinner, I faced Anne in the library.

"Why not let things be as they are, Anne?" I asked. "It can do no good. Whatever it is, and I do not know, why not let things rest?"

"Some one may find it," she replied. "Some one who does not care, as I—as we care."

"Are you sure there is something?"

"She told me, near the last. I only don't know just where it is."

"And if you find it?"

"It is a letter. I shall burn it without reading. Although," she drew a long breath, "I know what it contains."

"If in any way it comes into my hands," I assured her, "I shall let you know. And I shall not read it."

She looked thoughtful rather than grateful.

"I hardly know," she said. "I think she would want you to read it if it came to you. It explains so much. And it was a part of her plan. You know, of course, that she had a plan. It was a sort of arrangement"—she hesitated—"it was a sort of pact she made with God, if you know what I mean."

That night Maggie found the letter.

I had gone upstairs, and Anne was, I think, already asleep. I heard what sounded like distant hammering, and I went to the door. Some one was in the library below. The light was shining out into the hall, and my discovery of that was followed almost immediately by the faint splintering of wood. Rather outraged than alarmed, I went back for my dressing-gown, and as I left the room, I confronted Maggie in the hallway. She had an envelope in one hand, and a hatchet in the other.

"I found it," she said briefly.

She held it out, and I took it. On the outside, in Miss Emily's writing, it said, "To whom it may concern." It was sealed.

I turned it over in my hand, while Maggie talked.

"When I saw that girl crawling around," she said, "seems to me I remembered all at once seeing Miss Emily, that day I found her, running her finger along the baseboard. Says I to myself, there's something more hidden, and she don't know where it is. But I do. So I lifted the baseboard, and this was behind it."

Anne heard her from her room, and she went out soon afterward. I heard her going down the stairs and called to her. But she did not answer. I closed the door on Maggie and stood in my room, staring at the envelope.

I have wondered since whether Miss Emily,

had she lived, would have put the responsibility
on Providence for the discovery of her pitiful
story. So many of us blame the remorseless hand
of destiny for what is so manifestly our own
doing. It was her own anxiety, surely, that led to
the discovery in each instance, yet I am certain
that old Emily Benton died, convinced that a
higher hand than any on earth had directed the
discovery of the confession.

Miss Emily has been dead for more than a year
now. To publish the letter can do her no harm. In
a way, too, I feel, it may be the fulfilment of that
strange pact she made. For just as discovery was
the thing she most dreaded, so she felt that by
paying her penalty here she would be saved
something beyond—that sort of spiritual book-
keeping which most of us call religion. Anne
Sprague—she is married now to Martin has, I
think, some of Miss Emily's feeling about it,
although she denies it. But I am sure that in
consenting to the recording of Miss Emily's story,
she feels that she is doing what that gentle fatalist
would call following the hand of Providence.

I read the letter that night in the library where
the light was good. It was a narrative, not a letter,
strictly speaking. It began abruptly.

"I must set down this thing as it happened. I
shall write it fully, because I must get it off my

mind. I find that I am always composing it, and that my lips move when I walk along the street or even when I am sitting in church. How terrible if I should some day speak it aloud. My great-grandmother was a Catholic. She was a Bullard. Perhaps it is from her that I have this overwhelming impulse to confession. And lately I have been terrified. I must tell it, or I shall shriek it out some day, in the church, during the Litany. 'From battle and murder, and from sudden death, Good Lord, deliver us.'"

(There was a space here. When the writing began again, time had elapsed. The ink was different, the writing more controlled.)

"What a terrible thing hate is. It is a poison. It penetrates the mind and the body and changes everything. I, who once thought I could hate no one, now find that hate is my daily life, my getting up and lying down, my sleep, my waking.

"'From hatred, envy, and malice, and all uncharitableness, Good Lord, deliver us.'

"Must one suffer twice for the same thing? Is it not true that we pay but one penalty? Surely we pay either here or beyond, but not both. Oh, not both!

"Will this ever be found? Where shall I hide it? For I have the feeling that I must hide it, not destroy it— as the Catholic buries his sin with the priest. My father once said that it is the healthful humiliation of the confessional that is its reason for existing. If humiliation be a virtue—"

I have copied the confession to this point, but I find I can not go on. She was so merciless to herself, so hideously calm, so exact as to dates and hours. She had laid her life on the table and dissected it—for the Almighty!

I heard the story that night gently told, and somehow I feel that that is the version by which Miss Emily will be judged.

"If humiliation be a virtue—" I read and was about to turn the page, when I heard Anne in the hall. She was not alone. I recognized Doctor Lingard's voice.

Five minutes later I was sitting opposite him, almost knee to knee, and he was telling me how Miss Emily had come to commit her crime. Anne Bullard was there, standing on the hearth rug. She kept her eyes on me, and after a time I realized that these two simple people feared me, feared for Miss Emily's gentle memory, feared that I—good heaven!—would make the thing public.

"First of all, Miss Blakiston," said the doctor, "one must have known the family to realize the situation—its pride in its own uprightness. The virtue of the name, what it stood for in Bolivar County. She was raised on that. A Benton could do no wrong, because a Benton would do no wrong.

"But there is another side, also. I doubt if any

girl was ever raised as Miss Emily was. She—well, she knew nothing. At fifty she was as childlike and innocent as she was at ten. She had practically never heard of vice. The ugly things, for her, did not exist.

"And, all the time, there was a deep and strong nature underneath. She should have married and had children, but there was no one here for her to marry. I," he smiled faintly, "I asked for her myself, and was forbidden the house for years as a result.

"You have heard of the brother? But of course you have. I know you have found the books. Such an existence as the family life here was bound to have its reactions. Carlo was a reaction. Twenty-five years ago he ran away with a girl from the village. He did not marry her. I believe he was willing at one time, but his father opposed it violently. It would have been to recognize a thing he refused to recognize. He turned suddenly to Anne. "Don't you think this is going to be painful?" he asked.

"Why? I know it all."

"Very well. This girl—the one Carlo ran away with—determined to make the family pay for that refusal. She made them actually pay, year by year. Emily knew about it. She had to pinch to make the payments. The father sat in a sort of detached position, in the center of Bolivar County, and let her bear the brunt of it. I shall never forget the day she learned there was a child. It—well, it sickened her. She had not known about those things. And I imagine, if we could know, that that was the beginning of things.

"And all the time there was the necessity for secrecy. She had never known deceit, and now she was obliged to practice it constantly. She had no one to talk to. Her father, beyond making entries of the amounts paid to the woman in the case, had nothing to do with it. She bore it all, year after year. And it ate, like a cancer.

"Remember, I never knew. I, who would have done anything for her—she never told me. Carlo lived hard and came back to die. The father went. She nursed them both. I came every day, and I never suspected. Only, now and then, I wondered about her. She looked burned. I don't know any other word.

"Then, the night after Carlo had been buried, she telephoned for me. It was eleven o'clock, She met me, out there in the hall, and she said, 'John, I have killed somebody.'

"I thought she was out of her mind. But she opened the door, and—"

He turned and glanced at Anne.

"Please!" she said.

"It was Anne's mother. You have guessed it about Anne by now, of course. It seems that the funeral had taken the money for the payment that was due, and there had been a threat of exposure.

And Emily had reached the breaking-point. I believe what she said—that she had no intention even of striking her. You can't take the act itself. You have to take twenty-five years into account. Anyhow, she picked up a chair and knocked the woman down. And it killed her." He ran his fingers through his heavy hair. "It should not have killed her," he reflected. "There must have been some other weakness, heart or something. I don't know. But it was a heavy chair. I don't see how Emily—"

His voice trailed off.

"There we were," he said, with a long breath. "Poor Emily, and the other poor soul, neither of them fundamentally at fault, both victims."

"I know about the books," I put in hastily. I could not have him going over that again.

"You knew that, too!" He gazed at me.

"Poor Emily," he said. "She tried to atone. She brought Anne here, and told her the whole story. It was a bad time—all round. But at last Anne saw the light. The only one who would not see the light was Emily. And at last she hit on this confession idea. I suspected it when she rented the house. When I accused her of it, she said: "I have given it to Providence to decide. If the confession is found, I shall know I am to suffer. And I shall not lift a hand to save myself."

So it went through the hours. Her fear, which I still think was the terror that communicated itself to me; the various clues, which she, poor victim, had overlooked; the articles laid carelessly in the book she had been reading and accidentally hidden with her brother's forbidden literature; the books themselves, with all of five years to destroy them, and left untouched; her own anxiety about the confession in the telephone-box, which led to our finding it; her espionage of the house by means of the telephone; the doctor's night visit in search of the confession; the daily penance for five years of the dead woman's photograph in her room—all of these—and her occasional weakenings, poor soul, when she tried to change her handwriting against discovery, and refused to allow the second telephone to be installed.

How clear it was! How, in a way, inevitable! And, too, how really best for her it had turned out. For she had made a pact, and she died believing that discovery here had come, and would take the place of punishment beyond.

Martin Sprague came the next day. I was in the library alone, and he was with Anne in the garden, when Maggie came into the room with a saucer of crab-apple jelly.

"I wish you'd look at this," she said. "If it's cooked too much, it gets tough and—" She straightened suddenly and stood staring out through a window.

"I'd thank you to look out and see the goings-on in our garden," she said sharply. "In broad daylight, too. I—"

But I did not hear what else Maggie had to say. I glanced out, and Martin had raised the girl's face to his and was kissing her, gently and very tenderly.

And then—and again, as with fear, it is hard to put into words—I felt come over me such a wave of contentment and happiness as made me close my eyes with the sheer relief and joy of it. All was well. The past was past, and out of its mistakes had come a beautiful thing. And, like the fear, this joy was not mine. It came to me. I picked it up—a thought without words.

Sometimes I think about it, and I wonder—did little Miss Emily know?